To Bob Daly and Frank Dines, who are really great examples of what good friends are. And always, Stacey.—H.W.

For Oliver Baker, illustrious pitcher and beloved middle son.—L.O.

HANK ZIPZER

The World's Greatest Underachiever

The Zippity Zinger

by Henry Winkler and Lin Oliver

HANK ZIPZER

The World's Greatest Underachiever

The Zippity Zinger

Grosset & Dunlap • New York

Cover illustration by Jesse Joshua Watson

GROSSET & DUNLAP
Published by the Penguin Group
Penguin Group (USA) Inc., 375 Hudson Street, New York, New York 10014, U.S.A.
Penguin Group (Canada), 90 Eglinton Avenue East, Suite 700,
Toronto, Ontario, Canada M4P 2Y3
(a division of Pearson Penguin Canada Inc.)
Penguin Books Ltd, 80 Strand, London WC2R 0RL, England
Penguin Ireland, 25 St Stephen's Green, Dublin 2, Ireland
(a division of Penguin Books Ltd)
Penguin Group (Australia), 250 Camberwell Road, Camberwell,
Victoria 3124, Australia (a division of Pearson Australia Group Pty Ltd)
Penguin Books India Pvt Ltd, 11 Community Centre,
Panchsheel Park, New Delhi - 110 017, India
Penguin Group (NZ), Cnr Airborne and Rosedale Roads,
Albany, Auckland 1310, New Zealand (a division of Pearson New Zealand Ltd)
Penguin Books (South Africa) (Pty) Ltd, 24 Sturdee Avenue,
Rosebank, Johannesburg 2196, South Africa

Penguin Books Ltd, Registered Offices:
80 Strand, London WC2R 0RL, England

Text copyright © 2004 by Fair Dinkum and Lin Oliver Productions, Inc.
Cover illustration copyright © 2006 by Grosset & Dunlap.
Interior illustrations copyright © 2004 by Grosset & Dunlap. All rights reserved.
Published by Grosset & Dunlap, a division of Penguin Young Readers Group,
345 Hudson Street, New York, New York, 10014. GROSSET & DUNLAP is a
trademark of Penguin Group (USA) Inc. Printed in the U.S.A.

Library of Congress Control Number: 2003019216

ISBN-13: 978-0-448-43193-2 (pbk)   20 19 18 17 16 15 14 13 12

ISBN-13: 978-0-448-43287-8 (hc)   10 9 8 7 6 5 4

CHAPTER 1

"MOM! I'M OUT OF SOCKS," I called down the hall.

My sock drawer was totally empty. Okay, it wasn't *totally* empty. There were a few things in there, like a piece of red licorice left over from Halloween, a shoehorn that we used to jam my feet into a pair of size two dress-up shoes for my cousin's wedding, and a bunch of those little rainbow-colored rubber balls that bounce super high.

Anyway, the point I was getting to was that there were no socks in my drawer. This was serious because my grandpa, Papa Pete, was coming over to play catch and that's something you can't do sockless.

"Mom!" I hollered again. "I'm having a sock emergency."

My mom stuck her head in my room.

"What did you say, Hank? I can't hear you with these." She pointed to her ears. I wondered why she couldn't hear with her ears. What else would she hear with? Her nose?

I looked closer and realized that she was actually pointing to little headphones that she was wearing over her ears. You couldn't see them at first, because they were covered by her hair, which is blonde and curly and sticks out on the sides like earmuffs.

"What are you listening to?" I asked her in a loud voice.

"Crashing waves," she answered.

"Is that one of your eighties groups?"

"No, these are actual ocean waves crashing against rocks," she said.

Wow, and they say kids listen to weird music. At least you can dance to my stuff if you wanted to. Myself, I don't dance—at least, not in public.

"The waves get me in the mood for yoga class," my mom explained, "which, by the way, I'm late for."

She headed for the door.

"Wait, Mom, you can't leave now. I'm out of socks."

"You just noticed that?" she replied.

"No, I noticed yesterday, which is why I wore the same pair two days in a row."

"All your socks are in the wash," my mom said. "Just go pop them in the dryer and they'll be done in no time."

"I'm ten, Mom. I don't know how to just pop things in the dryer."

"It's easy, Hank," my mom said with a laugh. She thinks I'm funny even when I'm not trying to be. "Run down to the laundry room and take Emily's clothes out of the dryer, put them in the basket, and transfer your clothes from the washer to the dryer. There are four quarters on the kitchen table next to the Tide. You fit the quarters into the slots, push the whole thing in, and, presto, the machine starts. Is that all clear?"

"As glass, Mom. Laundry room, basket, quarters, slots. Got it."

My mom left for her class, which is held in my best friend Frankie Townsend's apartment, four floors down. His mom is a yoga teacher, and she's really good at it. She can bend all the way over and put her elbows on the floor. I tried that once, but I fell over on my head and split my pants right down the middle. It was pretty air-conditioned down there, if you know what I mean.

Mrs. Townsend has taught Frankie and me some really useful things, like how breathing deeply can help you relax when you're stressed. I did that when I took my last math test, and it really worked. I felt very relaxed—until I got my grade. There's something about getting an F that is extremely un-relaxing.

I checked the time. Papa Pete was coming in ten minutes, so I had to hurry. He was all excited about having a catch with me. To be honest, I wasn't so thrilled. I love to *watch* baseball, especially when my team, the New York Mets, is playing. But I'm not very good at *playing* it. In fact, I stink at it. And when I say stink, I don't mean I stink a little. I mean I stink-a-roony. I can't throw. I can't hit. And I can't field. Which just about covers everything that you'd ever have to do in baseball. It's embarrassing. Sometimes it seems that everyone in my class, my school, the world can play baseball, but me.

Papa Pete says all I need is a little practice. I

think all I need is a new set of arms and legs and a brain that makes them work correctly.

At first, I told Papa Pete that I didn't really want to have a catch. But then he said that he'd stop by my mom's deli, the Crunchy Pickle, to pick up some dills for us to eat afterwards. Pickles are our favorite snack. Sometimes, we sit outside on my balcony at night and munch down a whole bag of them. Papa Pete, who used to own the deli before he gave it to my mom to run, is an expert at picking out the crunchiest ones. So I guess the thought of those dark green, crunchy pickles won out over my lousy throwing arm, and I told Papa Pete to come on over.

The laundry room is in the basement of our apartment building. My friends and I have a clubhouse in the basement a few doors down from the laundry. I am so lucky that Frankie and my other best friend, Ashley Wong, live right in my building.

I took Cheerio, our crazed dachshund, with me to the basement. Not because I was scared or anything. You know, just for company. He can be really funny when he starts chasing his tail. He spins so fast that he actually looks like a Cheerio, which is how he got his name.

I got off the elevator and followed the scent of soapsuds to the laundry room. I walked in and there were the machines, just waiting for me.

What did my mom say? Take my sister Emily's clothes out of the dryer.

Done.

Put them in the white plastic basket and transfer mine from the washer into the dryer.

Done.

Did I remember the quarters for the machine?

Yes, I did. *Way to go, Hank.*

I'm not the best direction-follower in the world. In fact, I stink at that almost as much as I stink at baseball. No, maybe more, even. So I was pretty proud that I remembered everything my mom told me to do.

I started the dryer, picked up the white plastic basket, and plopped Cheerio on top of the warm clothes. He loves to sit on warm things. Then I ran to the elevator. I didn't want to keep Papa Pete waiting.

When I got back to our apartment, I put the basket down and reached for some socks.

"Hank Zipzer, you are a total moron!" I said out loud to myself.

I *still* had no socks. They were all in the dryer.

The doorbell rang and I heard Papa Pete's voice booming through the door.

"Is my favorite ballplayer ready?" he called. "Your number one fan is waiting for you."

"Just a second, Papa Pete," I shouted.

Without thinking about it, I kicked off my slippers and grabbed the first pair of socks on top of the basket and put them on without really focusing on what I was doing.

As I slipped on my sneakers, I caught a glimpse of the socks on my feet.

Hank Zipzer, are these your feet? Because, if they are, you are about to die of embarrassment.

Let's be clear. I don't own red socks—and I certainly don't own red socks with pink monkeys stitched on them. But that's exactly what was on my feet. BRIGHT RED GIRL'S SOCKS WITH LITTLE PINK MONKEYS ON THEM!!!!

It was like my feet were on fire. I started

hopping up and down, trying to get those monkey socks off before they were stuck on me forever. I think I yelled—screamed, really. It was as if an invisible monster had made me pull them on.

Can you imagine if someone saw me with my sister's monkey socks on? We would have to move to another city. No, another state! No, across the country! I would have to change my name, dye my hair, maybe even wear a mask.

Those monkey socks were staring up at me, and I swear they were laughing.

CHAPTER 2

*TEN REASONS WHY I WOULDN'T BE
CAUGHT DEAD IN MY SISTER'S MONKEY
SOCKS (OR ANYONE ELSE'S MONKEY
SOCKS, EITHER)*

1. Monkeys should live in trees, not on your ankles.
2. Socks should be white, unless you're going to your cousin's wedding, and then your parents make you wear black ones.
3. I have never seen one player on the Mets wearing any member of the animal kingdom below his knees.
4. If Nick McKelty, the bully of our class, knew that I had even considered putting on red-and-pink monkey socks, he would say, "There's Monkey Boy," when

he saw me every day for the rest of my life.

5. Number four is such a horrible thought, it counts for number five, too.
6. When Nick McKelty gets tired of calling me Monkey Boy, he'll switch to saying, "Gonna eat bananas and hang from the lights by your tail?"
7. Actually, hanging from the lights sounds like fun, because I could drop banana peels on McKelty's head. (I know this isn't really a reason, but it sure is fun to think about.)
8. Let me remind you, these were *pink* monkeys on *red* socks. Is that not reason enough?

9.

10.

**I skipped nine and ten because my brain stopped thinking of reasons after number eight. It does that. There's no arguing with my brain. When it's done, it's done.

CHAPTER 3

BEFORE I OPENED THE DOOR, I looked through the peephole to make sure it was Papa Pete. If I stood on my tippy toes, I could just barely see a big, red blur in our hallway. Then a burst of garlic and vinegar fumes wafted under our door. It was Papa Pete in the hall, alright, wearing his red warm-up suit like he always does on Sundays, and carrying a bag of garlic dill pickles.

I twisted the top lock open and then the bottom one and Papa Pete flew into the apartment and closed the door behind him.

"Just in the nick of time," he said. "Mrs. Fink is trying to get me to come in for a piece of her cherry strudel."

Mrs. Fink is our next-door neighbor. She's always baking things for Papa Pete. Once, I heard my mom telling my dad that she thinks

Mrs. Fink wants to have a romance with Papa Pete. When I heard her say that, I covered up my ears and starting yelling "peas and carrots, peas and carrots" really loud to block out the rest of the conversation. Trust me, you would have done that, too. Mrs. Fink is really nice— it's just that she cruises around our hall always wearing a huge, pink bathrobe and *not always* wearing her false teeth. That fact alone pretty much puts the whole romance topic off-limits for me.

"Hankie, we are going to have a great day. Very productive!" Papa Pete said. He grabbed my cheek between his thumb and pointer finger, and pinched. "Have I ever told you how much I love this cheek and everything attached to it?" he said.

"Only about a million and ten times," I answered.

"Good, then make this the million and eleventh," he said. He laughed as he went into the kitchen and put the bag of pickles into the refrigerator.

"Are you ready? Let's go to the park!" he shouted from the kitchen.

"I can't leave the apartment, Papa Pete," I said. "No socks! They're still in the dryer downstairs."

"There is a solution to every problem," he said as he came back into the living room.

"Not to this one," I said. "The only socks I could find were these." I lifted my pants to show him Emily's red monkey socks.

"Do they fit?" he asked.

"They do," I answered. "So what?"

"So you'll wear them to the park. Your pants will hide them, and with your handsome face, who is going to look at your feet?"

"No way, Papa Pete. My body is not leaving this apartment. Period."

"Listen, Hankie. You want to learn to throw, right? Today is the day. I can feel it!"

"Do you know how many kids I know who will be at the park?" I shook my head. "No thanks, Papa Pete. I'm sorry you came all the way over here for nothing."

"Wait a minute," Papa Pete said, twisting his big mustache with his fingers. "Something tells me you're trying to wiggle out of this because you think you're not good at baseball."

I didn't answer.

"Hankie, I wouldn't lie to you. You're getting better every time we try."

"I catch like a five-year-old girl with a blind-fold on," I said. "Face it, Papa Pete, I'm no athlete and never will be."

"Didn't you tell me on the phone that your school was having a big softball game this week?" Papa Pete said.

"It's the School Olympiad. The tryouts are tomorrow for the softball team."

"Do you want to play?" he asked.

"Of course. It's my dream," I answered. "But I'm horrible. I'm not going to try out."

Papa Pete put his big hand on my head. "I want only positive thoughts running around in there. You won't succeed if you don't believe you can. Now, come, let's practice."

"You're forgetting about these," I said, pointing to the monkeys that were still staring up at me from my ankles. Papa Pete pointed his finger toward the ceiling and spun it around in a circle, which he does when he has a great idea.

"We'll have the catch in the courtyard out-side the basement door. We'll be alone. You can wear monkey socks or rhinoceros socks and no one will see. End of conversation."

Leave it to Papa Pete to figure it out in the best possible way. I ran to my room, picked up my mitt, and flew out the door.

Whoops! It was only when I pushed the button for the elevator that I realized I had forgotten something very important. I went back and opened the apartment door. Papa Pete was still standing there, tapping his foot.

"Did you forget something? Namely—me?" he said.

We went back into the hall and got in the elevator. Just as the door was closing, we caught sight of Mrs. Fink coming out of her apartment. She was carrying cherry strudel and her mouth was closed, so we couldn't really tell about her teeth.

Papa Pete grinned at me as the elevator door shut.

"Saved by baseball," he said. We laughed as we rode the elevator down to the courtyard.

CHAPTER 4

"RIGHT HERE," Papa Pete yelled, pounding his fist into the center of his glove. "Put it right here!"

We were alone in the courtyard. Our apartment building towered over us on three sides, and the fourth wall was formed by the bricks of the building right next to ours. It was quiet there, and peaceful. The courtyard was starting to fill up with the smells of all the Sunday dinners cooking. I was pretty sure Mrs. Park was making Korean barbequed ribs, and I thought I smelled Mr. Grasso's sausage and peppers cooking on top of his stove. On Sundays, Ashley's grandmother always makes the greatest soups with wontons and pork and Chinese cabbage floating around like delicious little boats. I was wondering how wontons float when I suddenly realized that Papa Pete was talking to me.

"Hank, where are you?" he said. "Are we going to play ball or are we going to day-dream?"

"Sorry, Papa Pete, I was thinking about wonton boats," I said.

Papa Pete came over to me and put his hand on my shoulder.

"You've got to clear your brain of everything but the ball," he said. "The key to throwing is concentration. You have to keep your eyes on the target and focus. Where your head goes, your body goes. Where your body goes, your arm goes. And where your arm goes, the ball goes. It's that simple."

"Simple for you," I said. "Obviously, you can't smell Mrs. Wong's wontons."

"One thing at a time," said Papa Pete. "Play ball now. Eat wontons later." He handed me the ball. "Keep your eye on the center of my glove and let one rip."

Papa Pete walked back to the other side of the courtyard and squatted down like a catcher behind the metal drain we were using for home plate. I adjusted the ball in my hand.

Okay, here goes nothing.

I stared at Papa Pete's glove, brought my arm back behind my ear, whipped it around like a windmill, and released the ball. I was expecting my usual throw, which barely makes it to home plate.

Bam! The ball shot out of my hand and fired right into Papa Pete's glove. It was fast and hard and straight.

"What was that?" I said in amazement.

"Holy moly, Hankie!" Papa Pete said, and without saying another word, threw the ball right back to me.

He put his glove up again. I took the ball, wound up, and let it go underhand. *BAM!* The ball shot out of my hand and headed straight for the center of his glove . . . again.

"Excuse me, Mr. Professional," Papa Pete said. "Did you take a throwing pill this morning?"

"No! I don't know what's happening," I said. I looked down at my sneakers.

There they were. My sister's red socks, the monkeys half hidden by my pants. A thought ran through my head.

"Hey, Papa Pete! Throw me the ball,

please," I shouted. "I want to see something."

It couldn't be. No . . . it's not possible.

Papa Pete tossed me the ball, and I held it in my hand. I twisted it around so the stitching was directly on my fingertips.

Papa Pete squatted and put his mitt out in front of him. "Don't aim. Just throw."

I wound up like the last time and let the ball go. It flew across the courtyard and smashed dead center into Papa Pete's mitt. I wasn't doing anything different than I always did when we practiced in the park. Same windup. Same throw. Except this time I was throwing smoke. Why? There was only one thing that was different.

It must be! It's got to be! The socks!

"Hankie, I told you today was the day!" Papa Pete said. "I knew you could do this."

I was so excited. I was speechless. I had really thrown the ball and it really got to exactly where I wanted it to go.

There are no words to describe the thrill that was rushing through my body. I vowed never to forget the feeling. I kept on throwing to Papa Pete. I didn't want to stop. Ten throws. Twenty throws. Almost every one straight and accurate and fast. Nolan Ryan, Satchel Paige, Cy Young, Sandy Koufax. Step aside, gentlemen, and make way for Hank Zipzer. The man with the arm of steel.

Suddenly, the door to the courtyard flew open and Ashley and Frankie came running out.

"Hank!" Ashley said, pushing her glasses back on her nose. "I can't believe my eyes."

"You've been holding out on us, Zip," Frankie said, slapping me a high five. "Why did you tell us you can't throw? That's not what I see."

"We were upstairs helping my grandma chop vegetables for soup," Ashley said. "And we heard this *bam, bam, bam*. We looked out the window, and saw you throwing strikes. Hank, where have you been hiding that?"

"Honestly, guys," I said. "I've never thrown like this before. I don't know what's got into me." I couldn't tell them about the socks. They'd think I had gone nuts.

Papa Pete walked across the courtyard and came over to Frankie and Ashley. He pinched both of their cheeks.

"How are my grandkids?" he said. Even though they're not his grandkids, he calls them that and they love it. Every kid on the planet would want to be Papa Pete's grandchild, that is, every kid who likes lollipops and root-beer floats and big hugs and free tokens for video games.

"How do you like the arm on this boy?" Papa Pete asked, giving me one of those big hugs I just mentioned.

"Zipparooney, you throw like a Yankee," Frankie said.

"Correction. I throw like a Met," I answered. It's amazing that Frankie and I have remained best friends, even though he's a Yankees fan and I'm a Mets fan.

"Whoever you throw like, I want you to pitch for my team in the Olympiad," said Ashley.

"What team is that?" asked Papa Pete.

"The Yellow Team." Ashley turned to Papa Pete. "You're looking at the first female manager of an Olympiad softball team in the history of PS 87," she said proudly.

"My hat is off to you," said Papa Pete, taking off his hat and saluting Ashley. "I always knew you'd be a big shot someday."

"Hi, guys," said a nasal little voice from behind us. It was Robert Upchurch, third-grade nuisance. He had spotted us. No matter where we are in the building, Robert will sniff us out like a mouse smells cheese and want to join in. He's like our shadow. A very bony, long-winded, nose-blowing shadow.

"Perhaps you'd all enjoy it if I gave you a brief history of the Olympiad," Robert said.

"Perhaps you can skip it, dude," Frankie said. But once Robert has it in his mind to tell you about something, you have no choice but to wait it out. The boy has got a brain like a tape recorder, and once he's on "play," there's no shutting him off.

"The Olympiad is an all-school competition now in its twenty-seventh year at PS 87. Everyone in the third grade or above is either put on the Yellow Team or the Blue Team," Robert droned on. The kid was on autopilot. We all started to yawn, but that didn't stop old Robert. No, sir.

"We participate in three events to test our mind, body, and spirit. The softball game is the traditional test of the body, the Brain Buster Quiz is our mind test, and the Triple C Competition is the spirit test."

"Triple C, that sounds serious," said Papa Pete.

"Actually, it is extremely serious," said Robert. "It stands for Clean and Clutter-Free Competition. Last year, Terry Sladnick set a school record in this event by washing her hair every day of the school year, including weekends, without getting even one split end. Now that's what I call clean and clutter-free."

"Are you finished with the lecture, Robert?" Ashley said. "Because I have business to discuss with Hank."

"Actually," said Robert. "I have more to say."

"Actually, you don't," said Frankie, "because if you do, I'll have to tie your lips together with a red ribbon and give them away for Christmas."

"Hank," Ashley said, putting her business face on. Ashley is the business manager of our magic group, Magik 3, and we picked her for that job because when she means business, she means business. "I want you to pitch for the Yellow Team. You'll be our secret weapon."

"Let me take your temperature, Ash," I said. "That's the craziest thing I've ever heard. You have to trust me. Today was an accident."

"Come on, Hank. If you did it once, you can do it again," Ashley pleaded.

"I agree," added Papa Pete. "I've been telling him there is a wonderful baseball player inside him, just waiting to come out."

"Well, say hello," Frankie said, "because he just arrived."

Even though Frankie and Ashley are my best friends, I just couldn't tell them the truth. It sounded too crazy. One minute, I'm the worst ball thrower in history. The next minute, I throw like I'm on fire. And the reason is that I'm wearing my sister's red monkey socks. You see, that sounds crazy even to me and I'm the one who's saying it.

"Hey, I just remembered that my clothes are in the dryer," I said. "I gotta go, guys. See you later."

"Hank?!" Ashley called out as I bolted for the door.

"Can't do it, Ashley," I shouted back without turning around.

Papa Pete, Ashley, and Frankie just stood there staring at one another.

Just as the door to the building closed behind me, I heard Papa Pete say, "I'll talk to him."

"Well, good luck," Frankie answered. "I know Zip, and he doesn't sound like he's in a listening mood."

CHAPTER 5

WHILE WE ATE OUR CRUNCHY DILLS that afternoon, Papa Pete tried to talk me into pitching for the Yellow Team. I said no. With or without monkey socks, a guy knows his limits.

I don't know if I've mentioned this before, but I have learning challenges. Certain things in school are really hard for me, like reading and math and spelling. And certain things out of school are hard for me, too, like throwing and catching. There are so many things to concentrate on that my mind just sort of goes blank. My mind and my hands don't seem to like each other. They sure don't listen to each other.

I'm not bad at all sports. My best sport is archery, which I did at camp last summer. I even won a Master Archer pin for hitting ten bull's-eyes in a row. Too bad I don't live in Robin Hood's time. I would have been such a cool dude, running around in those green tights, shooting off my bow and arrow to protect people. Cool dudes with bows and arrows aren't too welcome on the Upper West Side of Manhattan these days.

After Papa Pete left, I went to my room to study for my social studies test. I was lying on my bunk bed with my headphones on and my book on the Hopi Indians open next to me. There was a really interesting picture of the oldest house in America that was built for the chief of the Hopi over one thousand years ago. I stared at the picture, thinking about all the things they didn't have way back then—toilets, skateboards, striped toothpaste, cell phones, Pop-Tarts. Of course, even if they did have Pop-Tarts, they couldn't have eaten them because they didn't have toasters, either.

"Hank! How many times do I have to call you?" I could hear my dad yelling through the headphones. He tapped me on the shoulder and I nearly jumped out of my skin.

"Don't do that, Dad. You scared me!"

"I've been calling you for the last five minutes," he said.

"I was studying."

"With headphones on?" he said. "You shouldn't be listening to music while you're studying. How many times do I have to tell you that?"

"I'm not listening to music," I said. "Here, listen for yourself."

I handed my dad the earphones and he put them on.

"What is this?" he asked.

"It's Dr. Berger, reading from our social studies book."

Dr. Berger is the learning specialist at my school, and she works with me sometimes to figure out how I can best study my way. She is really nice, and doesn't think I'm even a little bit stupid.

"She recorded some Hopi facts for me to listen to," I told my dad. "She thinks maybe they'll stick in my head better if I listen to them while I'm looking at the book."

"Sounds like that would be more confusing," my dad said. "If the TV is on when I'm doing a crossword puzzle, I can't concentrate on either of them."

"It's working for me, Dad," I said. "I know so much about the Hopi that I didn't know ten minutes ago. Like did you know that—"

"Save it for the table," my dad interrupted. "Dinner's ready."

"What are we having?"

I always ask that question with some fear, and I have a good reason for that. My mom is what you'd call an experimental cooker. At her deli, the Crunchy Pickle, her goal is to bring lunch meats into the twenty-first century. So, instead of making salami and corned beef the regular way, she makes them out of tofu and soy and a bunch of other low-fat, low-taste things. At home, our kitchen is her science lab. She'll whip up a leek and soy-milk soufflé at the drop of a hat, and then throw in a side of mock tuna with bean sprouts just for fun. Most of her dishes taste like what I imagine paper tastes like.

"It looks like lasagna," my dad whispered, "but I don't know what Mom has planted under that top layer of noodle. I do know this: The noodles are made from wheatgrass."

"Do we have to mow them before we eat them?" I asked.

That made my dad laugh, which is not something that happens every day. Or even every week.

We sat down at the dining room table, which is actually the part of the living room that we call the dining room. It was the five of us Zipzers. That would be my mom, the lovely Randi Zipzer; my dad, Stan; my nine-year-old sister Emily; and let's not forget her not-so-lovely iguana, Katherine. Katherine was wrapped around Emily's neck like a scaly scarf.

I don't usually love it when Katherine joins us for meals. First of all, looking at a scaly face when you're eating doesn't do much for the old appetite. And, second of all, she has this long grey tongue that shoots out onto your plate and steals the best part of your dinner. If there is a best part, that is.

My mom cut into her green lasagna experiment, and put a huge helping the size of Montana on my plate.

"Dig in, everyone," she said with a big smile. She looked so happy with her creation.

I dug in. My fork went in and found what was buried under the wheatgrass noodle. I don't know what it was, but let me just say this: Whatever it was made the wheatgrass noodle look delicious by comparison. It was dark brown with flecks of black. And it was oozing.

"What's this, Mom?" I asked. I was afraid of the answer. Very afraid.

"Mushroom puree with crushed blue-berries," she answered. "Taste it, honey."

All eyes were on me. I put some of the mushroom puree on my fork and shoved it in my mouth quickly. I've found that if you don't breathe while chewing, you don't really taste what's in your mouth. I didn't breathe. I chewed and swallowed and took a big gulp of milk. Then I smiled at my mom who was wait-ing for my comment.

"Wow," I said, trying to sound enthusiastic. "Wow, wow, wow."

"I knew you'd like it." My mom smiled.

I looked over at Katherine and when my mom wasn't looking, slipped her a big bite of the lasagna. She shot her long tongue out, and faster than you could say "I'm going to barf now," her tongue sprang back in her mouth and she buried her head in Emily's hair. I looked under the table for Cheerio.

"I hate to do this to you, boy," I whispered, "but I'm a desperate man."

I held a bite of the lasagna in my hand and slipped it under the table. Cheerio took one sniff and started spinning around in circles. He actually spun himself out from under the table, across the living room, and over to the front door. He wanted out, and I didn't really blame him.

"So, Hank, how's your studying going?" my mom asked.

"Great, Mom. My brain is getting so full of information about the Hopi."

"It doesn't take much to fill up your pea brain," said Emily. She is really smart, the total opposite of me, but I wasn't going to let her get away with that remark.

"Hey, Emily," I said. "I'll bet you don't know how many kinds of corn the Hopi Indians grew."

"Seven," she said in her Miss Know-It-All voice.

"Twenty-four," I answered. It's not often I know something Emily doesn't know, so I went in for the kill.

"I'll bet you don't know what a *kiva* is," I grilled her.

"A chocolate bar from Switzerland," she said.

"Hey, so close, yet so far," I said. "It's an underground room that you can only get to by ladder where the Hopi built fires and had their religious ceremonies and sweated a lot."

"That's great, Hank." Emily made a face at me. "Now can we talk about something interesting, like the digestive system of the gecko?" Emily is a major reptile person. As if you couldn't tell.

"Emily, let Hank tell us about the Hopi tribe," my mom said. "He's doing such a nice job studying for his test tomorrow."

"I didn't know you could learn so much just listening to a tape," I said. "Like, did you know that the Hopi think of themselves as caretakers of the Earth? They believe you can't own the land, but you have to share it with everybody. And they make these dolls called *kachinas* and they use them to pray for rain and other things they need."

"Who doesn't know about *kachinas*?" Emily said.

"Oh, really. Then what kind of wood are they made out of?" I said.

"I know," Emily answered. "I'm just not in the mood to say."

"As if cottonwood was right on the tip of your tongue," I said.

"Honestly, Hank, you learn three little facts and you think you're so smart," Emily said. "Those of us who are going to be on the Brain Buster Team in the Olympiad have to know a million things like that."

Everyone stopped eating and looked at Emily.

"Em, sweetheart, I didn't know you had been chosen for the Brain Buster Team!" my dad said. He gave her a big kiss on the cheek, barely missing Katherine, who stuck her snout out to get in on the action.

"My teacher strongly suggested that I lead the Blue Team to victory by becoming a Brain Buster," Emily said, glancing over at me with her smarty pants look. "I was the first third-grader they asked."

My dad smiled so big you could see that the wheatgrass had gotten stuck between almost every tooth.

"Oh, yeah? Well I have some Olympiad news myself," I said before I even knew what was coming out of my mouth. "I am going to pitch for the Yellow Softball Team."

I was? Hank Zipzer, stop your mouth. Stop it right now.

My mouth wasn't listening, though. It went right on.

"Yeah, Ashley and Frankie were practically begging me today. They saw me throwing with Papa Pete in the courtyard and I was on fire."

My dad picked up his glass of water with lemon wedges and held it up.

"Here's to my two Olympians," he said, and took a big gulp.

"This pitching thing, that's a very exciting change for you, isn't it?" my mom said.

"I never missed the center of Papa Pete's glove. I was having a lucky day," I said, taking a swig of my milk.

"Oh, speaking about lucky," Emily said. "Mom, remind me to make sure I wear my lucky monkey socks on Tuesday for the Olympiad."

I nearly choked on my milk. *Did she just say what I think she said?*

"What do they look like?" I asked.

"The red socks with the pink monkeys stitched on them," Emily said. "They always bring me luck. I wore them when I got one hundred percent plus ten extra-credit points on my math test. And I wore them when I got the solo part in the Winter Sing. And . . . "

I didn't hear the rest of what she said. All I could do was look very slowly, so that no one would notice, down at my feet, which were covered in my sister's lucky monkey socks.

Maybe they *really were* the reason I could suddenly pitch.

No, it couldn't be.

No way.

CHAPTER 6

AFTER DINNER, I TRIED to go back to studying for my social studies test. I had already finished listening to the tape, so I picked up my book and looked at the pictures. It had a whole page of pictures of *kachina* dolls. One was wearing moccasins with tiny beads. Another one had a cape made out of rabbit fur. In one hand he had a big spear, and in the other he was holding an orange, black, and yellow shield covered in feathers. But no matter how long I stared at those pictures, all I kept seeing were monkey faces on each doll.

I've learned that when I have a powerful problem in my brain, it hangs around in there and takes up all my thinking space until I deal with it. I definitely had monkey socks on the brain, which isn't very comfortable, so I decided to deal with it.

I dialed Frankie's number. You know when you really want to talk to someone, how it seems like the phone rings forever? That's what happened. It felt like it took fifteen rings before Frankie's dad answered.

"Hello, Dr. Townsend," I said.

"Ah, it's the young Mr. Zipzer," he said. "Always a pleasure to hear your mellifluous voice on the phone."

"Thank you, sir."

I had no idea what I was thanking him for. He's a professor of African-American Studies at Columbia University and he uses words that are a block long. They're so long, I don't even know how he gets them all out in one breath.

"Frankie was just talking about you at dinner. He said you're developing quite a rotation on the pitched ball."

"Thank you," I said again. This time, I thought I actually understood him.

"When did this nascent talent of yours emerge?" he said.

"Dr. Townsend, I would love to um . . . conversate with you," I said, "but I've got a situation that demands Frankie, so could we conversate later?"

"I understand the immediacy of your predicament," he said.

I was hoping that meant good-bye. It must have, because he put down the phone and called for Frankie.

"Talk to me, Zip," said Frankie, which is his standard way of saying hello.

"Are you busy right now?" I said, sounding a little desperate even to myself. "I've got to come down and see you."

"Zip, I'm studying for the social studies test, which you should be doing, too."

"I'm trying, but all I see are monkeys."

"There are no monkeys on the Hopi reservation, my man. Never have been. Never will be."

"No, Frankie, the monkeys are in my head."

"I don't like the sound of this," he said. "Get down here right away. You need me."

I left the apartment so fast that if I were a comic-book character, you'd have seen streaks behind my feet. I didn't wait for the elevator. I took the back stairs.

Frankie was waiting for me at the door of his apartment. I flew past him, went straight to his room, and then realized I hadn't told my parents I was leaving.

"Can I use your phone?" I asked.

"Are you calling any monkeys?"

"No. Just my dad."

He handed me his phone, and I called home to say where I was. Then I hung up and turned to Frankie.

"Ground rules," I began. "You can't laugh."

"About what?"

"About these." Slowly, I pulled up my jeans to reveal the red-and-pink monkey socks wrapped around my ankles. Frankie bit his lower lip.

"Okay, I'm not laughing," he said, "but I am requesting permission to grin. You have to admit, Hank, they're funny. Now here's an important question. Think before you answer."

"Okay," I said.

"What are those socks doing on your feet?"

"All my socks were in the washing machine," I began. "Actually, they were in the dryer, but they were there because they had just been in the washing machine."

"Zip, I know how the laundry room works," said Frankie. "Now get to the point. Those socks, your feet."

"Papa Pete was coming to play catch with me, and I had to put something on. My socks were drying, so I grabbed the first socks on top of the laundry basket. I wasn't paying attention."

"As usual."

"And then I threw strikes like I've never thrown before."

"Yeah, you were throwing some real heat."

"Then at dinner, Emily says she's got to wear her lucky monkey socks because she's going to be in the Brain Buster at the Olympiad. I nearly choked on my wheatgrass. I kept thinking what if, but then I thought, no, couldn't be."

"Couldn't be what?" Frankie scratched his head, running his hand over his curly black hair.

"That these really *are* lucky socks. They've brought Emily all kinds of luck, and now they're working for me, too. Tell me, Frankie, does that sound totally crazy?"

"It makes all kinds of sense to me," Frankie

said. "Listen, Zip, almost every athlete has something that's a lucky charm. Turk Wendell, he used to be on your stinkin' Mets . . ."

"Number ninety-nine. What about him?"

"He brushes his teeth and chews licorice between every inning."

"I didn't know that."

"Wade Boggs . . ."

"Formerly on your stinkin' Yankees, then on the Devil Rays, now retired."

"Yup. That guy ate nothing but chicken on game day for his whole career. One slice of pizza and he would've been hitting like your sister's iguana."

"What about socks? Does anyone have any lucky socks?"

I hadn't even finished the question before Frankie was on the Internet, typing in the words "sports superstitions." His computer screen came alive with words as thick as ants.

"Check this out," Frankie said, pointing to the screen.

When words are that close together and there are so many of them, I can't quite make sense of them. I think I'll never be able to read them, even before I try.

"Just read it to me," I said. Frankie nodded. He never makes me feel stupid. We've known each other too long for that.

"There's a million things listed here," Frankie said. "Everybody's got some lucky charm that works for him. Here's a guy who's got to wear a Jetsons T-shirt under his uniform for every game. Here's another one who sticks a wad of gum under his hat for luck. And look at all these players who don't shave. When you're on a winning streak, don't even think about shaving."

"I don't," I said.

"And this guy, Mark 'The Bird' Fidrych, used to talk to the ball before every pitch."

"What did he say?"

"I don't know," Frankie answered. "But what are you going to say to a ball? Strike the sucker out."

"So, Frankie, what you're telling me is that these things actually bring people luck."

"It's right here," he said, pointing at the screen.

I looked down at the red-and-pink monkey socks. Suddenly, they didn't look stupid. They looked beautiful to me. They were my lucky socks.

"So," Frankie said. "You got your good luck charm. And with me catching for you, we got the Yellow Team victory locked up. Problem solved, Zippola."

"You're right," I agreed. "Problem solved. Over. Finito."

We high-fived.

"Can I go back to studying now, Zip?"

"Yup. As soon as you tell me one thing."

"What's that?"

"How do I break the news to Emily that *her* lucky socks are now *mine*?"

CHAPTER 7

When I went to bed that night, I hid the monkey socks in my third drawer, right in between my Mets sweatshirt and my Spider-Man boxers.

Okay, I confess. I was hiding them from Emily.

The next morning, all I could think about were those lucky monkey socks. I wanted to keep them more than I've ever wanted anything. If I could just have those socks for a couple of days, I could pitch at the Olympiad. I could lead the Yellow Team to victory. And, for once, I could make Nick the Tick McKelty, who has been picking on me since the day I was born, show me some respect.

I was imagining how great that would feel, and eating my Captain Munch-a-Crunch cereal, when my mom walked in.

"Hank, I put some sardines out for you," she said. "Why aren't you eating them?"

"Because sardines are slimy, smelly, and let's face it, Mom, revolting."

"But, honey, the fatty fish oils are brain food. Think how they'll help you on your social studies test."

My social studies test! I had completely forgotten about it. Maybe I *am* stupid. How could I listen to an entire book on tape, take notes on both blue and yellow index cards, and still wake up and have completely forgotten that I have a test today?

Maybe my mom was right. Maybe I do need fatty fish oils. I looked over at the plate of sardines. *No,* I thought. *I can't eat those.* My taste buds would stand up and walk right off my tongue and never come back.

These horrible thoughts were running through my brain when Emily came into the kitchen and sat down for breakfast.

"Wow, Mom! Sardines! What a treat. Katherine and I love them."

She picked up one of the slimy little fish, split it in two, popped half in her mouth, and fed the other half to Katherine.

"You have some fatty fish oil on your face," I said, handing her a napkin. "Better wipe it off or it will ruin your social life. People will smell your face a mile away."

"Mom," Emily called out, ignoring me as usual. "Have you seen my lucky monkey socks? I've looked all over for them and I still can't find them."

I got very busy with my cereal, hoping that Emily wouldn't see the panic that jolted through my body.

"Did you check the laundry basket?" Mom asked.

"They're not there."

"The sock drawer? The hamper? Under your bed?"

"Of course I did," answered Emily. "I'm not Hank."

"Honey, I've got to get to the deli. Can I look for them later? Do you have to have them now?"

"Not really," answered Emily. "Today is only the tryouts for the Brain Buster Team and I won't have any trouble making it. But I'll need them tomorrow for the Olympiad. Hank, you haven't seen them, have you?"

My cereal bubbled up in my throat.

"Hey, look at the time," I said. "I've got to run."

And I did. Straight to my room and closed the door.

Breathe, Hank. Think this through.

True, they are Emily's socks. And I guess the right thing to do is to give them back to her. On the other hand, she doesn't really need them. She's good at everything. She'll do fine in the Olympiad, whether she has the monkey socks or not.

"Hank," my dad called from the living room. "Time to leave. You don't want to be late for your test."

My test. If the socks helped Emily get 110 percent on her math test, then maybe they'd help me out on my social studies test, so I could get rid of that D on my report card.

I'll just use them today. Just long enough to bring my grade up.

I went to the drawer and pulled the socks from their hiding place. When I slipped them on, I realized they could be seen from under my jeans. This was going to require camouflage. I pulled another pair of plain white socks from my drawer, slid them on my feet, and pulled them up to hide the monkeys.

With two pairs of socks on, my shoes were so tight, I had to loosen the laces to get them on. I grabbed my jacket, left my room, and flew out into the living room where my dad was waiting to walk us to school.

"Backpack," my dad said.

"Right," I answered.

I flew back into my room and took my backpack from my desk chair. I forget to take it sometimes. A lot of times. Okay, every day.

As I headed toward the front door, Katherine appeared out of nowhere. She held very still for a split second and appeared to be sniffing the air. Her beady eyes zeroed in on me—on my feet. She must have smelled Emily on my socks, because she scurried across the floor and grabbed onto my ankles. I'm not kidding, she dug her little claws into my socks and hung on like she was riding a skateboard.

"Get off me," I whispered to Katherine. I

shook my leg really hard, but she hung on. Then what I didn't want to happen happened. Emily noticed.

"That's strange," she said. "Katherine usually hates you."

"Not as much as I hate her," I said. "Now could you please remove this scaly lettuce-eater from my ankles so we can get to school?"

"Only if you lower your voice," Emily said. "Kathy gets stressed out from yelling."

"I'm going to use Kathy as a football if you don't unhinge her right now," I growled.

Emily bent down to lift Katherine off me.

"Your socks are so thick," she said.

I was hoping that those monkey socks would stay put under my white socks, right where I had hidden them.

Stay, boys. Don't fail me now.

I must've said that out loud, because Emily stopped what she was doing and looked at me.

"Did you say something to me?" she said.

"Why would I do that?" I answered.

It took a lot of work for Emily to get Katherine off me. She had to pry her disgusting little iguana claws out of my socks. There was actually one tiny red thread that attached itself to the third claw on Katherine's right front foot. Or maybe it was her left front foot—I'm not good with right and left. When I saw that red thread, my heart stopped. I could feel sweat starting to drip from my temples.

But Emily was so busy talking her drippy baby talk to Katherine that she didn't notice the red thread. The monkey socks stayed hidden.

Phew. That was too close for comfort.

CHAPTER 8

ON THE WAY TO SCHOOL, I gave the monkeys a pep talk.

I need you, boys. You got to give me everything you know about Native Americans, specifically Hopi. Pottery, *kachina* dolls, rain dances—let me have it all.

Hey, guys—here's a warm-up.

What year was the chief's house, the oldest house in America, built? 1145, you say? That's right. You're cooking now.

And they were. Those monkeys pulled me through.

I got a B-minus on the social studies test.

I don't know if a B-minus is a good grade to you, but let me tell you this: In the world of yours truly, Hank Daniel Zipzer, that is as good as a solid gold A.

Go, monkey socks!

CHAPTER 9

"DR. BERGER! DR. BERGER!" I yelled before I even got through her office door.

"Hey, slow down, Hank," said Ms. Halzal, the other special-education therapist. "Where's the fire?"

"Me. I'm on fire. I just have to talk to Dr. Berger. Is she here?"

"Dr. Lynn will be back in a minute. Have a seat," offered Ms. Halzal.

I sat down on one of the metal-legged chairs with a blue plastic seat, but I couldn't sit still. My knee was shaking up and down like it had a motor in it. After a second or two, I decided my butt was not comfortable so I slid over to the yellow seat. But I didn't stay long on that one either because Dr. Berger, who likes to be called Dr. Lynn, walked in. Without stopping, she said, "Nice to see you, Hank. Why don't you join me in my office?"

I got up and followed her into her office, which has these really great posters on the wall. One shows a basket overflowing with puppies. Every time I see them, I want to take one of them home. Then Cheerio would have a friend to chase, instead of his tail. And they both would keep Katherine in line.

"So, how did the book on tape work out?" Dr. Lynn asked.

"That's what I wanted to see you about," I said. "I have to tell you two important things. But you have to keep what I'm about to tell you a secret and please don't laugh."

"I think I can handle those requests," she said, smiling. "You're not going to tell me you got in trouble at home for listening instead of reading, are you?"

"No! No! Nothing like that. It's weirder." I took a deep breath. My insides felt like I could trust her.

"I got a B-minus on my Hopi test and do you know why?"

"Yes, I do. Because it is easier for you, Hank, to absorb information through your ears than through your eyes."

"Nope. It's the monkey socks," I blurted out.

Dr. Lynn raised an eyebrow and started playing with the pearls around her neck.

"It's because of my sister's lucky red socks with pink monkeys," I went on. "I put them on by mistake yesterday, and now look. I did really well on my social studies test, and I also threw a softball faster and straighter than I ever have in my whole entire life."

"Wait a second, Hank. Let's back up," Dr. Lynn said. There was a smile waiting to burst across her lips, but I saw her catch it before it turned into a laugh. She's a person who keeps her promises.

"You're telling me you think . . ."

"I know!" I interrupted. "I'm telling you . . . even Frankie said it was the lucky monkey socks. They have cured my learning problem. It's a miracle!"

"That sounds wonderful, Hank. But can we look at another possibility?" Dr. Lynn asked.

"Sure, Dr. Lynn. Lay it on me."

"Let's start with throwing the softball. Was there anything different about it?" she asked.

"Like where you were or what you did?"

"Just the place we played," I answered. "My grandpa suggested we play catch in the courtyard of our building and not in the park."

"Really. And why did he do that?" Dr. Lynn wanted to know.

"Because of the monkey socks," I whispered. "I didn't want anyone to see me in them and if we went to the park, everyone would."

"What does the courtyard look like?"

"Regular. A big square with building walls on all four sides," I answered.

"Is it closed off from the street?"

"Yes!" I said. "Have you ever been down there?"

"No, Hank, I haven't. But let's look at the possibility that because it's quiet and isolated, there were very few distractions to take your mind off your task at hand," Dr. Lynn explained. "You were able to concentrate on throwing."

"Now that I think of it, it was quiet down there. But you should have seen me pitch that ball. Amazing is what it was. No, Dr. Lynn, a pitch like that has to happen by magic. It was the socks. Besides, it has to be, because they worked again on the test."

"Hank, don't you see . . ."

The bell rang, which meant that lunch period was over and I had to get to class. My teacher, Ms. Adolf, sends you to Principal Love's office when you're late too many times.

"Thanks for listening, Dr. Lynn," I said as I raced out her office door. "Remember, you promised not to tell anyone. And a promise is sacred to the Hopi."

"I'll keep my promise, Hank, but we have to continue this conversation," Dr. Lynn called after me.

I charged down the hall to my class. I think the monkey socks were making me run even faster than usual.

Wow. They were powerful.

CHAPTER 10

As I slid into my seat, Ms. Adolf was already writing on the blackboard, listing the Olympiad teams and the event schedule for the next day. Her grey skirt, which she wears every single day to match her grey shirt and her grey shoes and her grey face, was smudged with chalk dust.

"Excuse me, Ms. Adolf," Luke Whitman said as he walked by her. "You have chalk poop on your butt."

You have to give Luke Whitman credit. He is not afraid to say what's on his mind. Everyone laughed at the chalk poop remark, and that made Ms. Adolf really mad. She thinks fourth-graders laugh too much to begin with, and laughing at her rear end is certainly not okay with her.

"Quiet, pupils," she said. "I see nothing

funny about a little chalk dust."

"You would, if you could see your butt," said Luke. "It's hilarious."

We couldn't help laughing again. I could see red splotches flaring up on Ms. Adolf's cheeks, which is a sign that she's steaming mad. She took off the silver key she wears on a lanyard around her neck and unlocked the top drawer of her desk. Picking up her roll book, she wrote a little note next to Luke's name and then took out the hall pass.

"I think you know where you're going with this," she said to Luke, handing him the hall pass.

"To the cafeteria for a snack?" said Luke.

"Absolutely not," said Ms. Adolf. "You just march to Principal Love's office. That's where pupils go who insist on talking about their teacher's hindquarters."

As Luke left the room, he looked at me and said, "I'll keep the seat warm for you."

I said a secret thank you that, this time, it wasn't me going to Principal Love's office. Believe me, I've spent plenty of time sitting across from Principal Love. Doing mole time, we call it. That's because Principal Love has this mole on his face that's shaped like the Statue of Liberty without the torch. When he talks to you, his mole shakes like crazy and it looks like the Statue of Liberty has ants in her pants. All you can do is stare at it while you're trying not to stare.

"These are the final teams for tomorrow's Olympiad," Ms. Adolf said, pointing to the blackboard. "Half of you have been assigned to the Yellow Team, and the other half is on the Blue Team. Check over the list on the board, and make sure that you have been assigned to the event you tried out for."

I looked at the board. Ashley was listed as the manager of the Yellow Softball Team. Frankie was a member of the team. Kim Paulson, the second most beautiful girl in our class, was on the Yellow Team, too, as was Ryan Shimozato, who is an awesome athlete. Nick McKelty, the single most obnoxious human being ever hatched, had been assigned to the Blue Softball Team. At least Frankie and Ashley weren't going to have to play on the same team as Nick the Tick.

My name was listed under the Triple C Competition. I enrolled for that event because, at the time, it was my only choice. I knew I couldn't play softball, and I certainly wasn't qualified to be on the Brain Buster Squad. So that left the Triple C Competition as the only event I even had a shot at. I happen to be really good at sharpening all the pencils in my desk so that they are exactly the same length. I thought that would impress the judges, for sure.

Ashley stuck her hand up in the air and Ms. Adolf called on her.

"Yes, Ms. Wong," she said.

"I'd like to request a change in teams," Ashley said. "As manager of the Yellow Softball Team, I am requesting that Hank Zipzer be transferred to my team."

"That's your first mistake, girlfriend!" shouted a voice from behind us. I didn't have to look. It was McKelty's voice. He's really loud and always sounds like he's laughing at you, which by the way, he usually is.

I poked Ashley across the aisle.

"What are you doing?" I whispered.

"Frankie told me about the socks," she

whispered back. "This is your lucky chance, so I went ahead and put you on the team."

"Ash, I can't."

"Hank, I saw you throw. You're dynamite."

Frankie's hand shot up.

"As the official catcher of the Yellow Team, I'd like to second Manager Wong's request for Zipzer. We'd like to draft him."

"Is this all right with you, Henry?" Ms. Adolf asked me. She is the only person in the world who calls me Henry, except for my mother when she's mad. Ms. Adolf doesn't believe in nicknames. She thinks they're unnecessary.

"Yes, Ms. Adolf, it's okay with him," Ashley said before I had a chance to speak up. "We've already discussed it."

"I can't believe you're drafting Zipper Boy!" snorted McKelty. "I wouldn't draft him for the toilet squad."

That's exactly the kind of thing Nick McKelty says all the time—it's just mean and creepy. A bunch of kids giggled.

That guy was making my blood boil, especially now that he had the class laughing. I looked down at my white socks and knew that the lucky monkey socks were underneath, just waiting to be used.

Why not? What are lucky socks good for, if not to put jerks like McKelty in their place?

"Hey, McKelty," I whispered. "Meet me on the athletic field after school. I've got something to show you."

"What's that, Zipper Face?" he snarled, blasting some of his bad breath over my way.

"Two words," I said. "Guess what they are?"

"Girly throw?" he said.

I shot him my most confident grin and whispered the two words.

"Secret weapon."

CHAPTER 11

AT EXACTLY THREE O'CLOCK, Frankie, Ashley, and I were on the athletic field, waiting at the baseball diamond that had been set up for the Olympiad. Robert Upchurch was there, too, for no particular reason except that he always gloms on to us and we can never shake him.

"Robert," Frankie said. "Go home."

"I'm on the Yellow Team, too," Robert said. "I have a right to be here."

"You're in the Triple C Competition," Ashley said. "Look around, Robert. This is a baseball diamond."

"Actually, it's a softball diamond," said Robert. "A baseball diamond has to meet regulation measurements. Would you like me to tell you what those are, because I have committed them to memory."

"No," we all said at once.

"Another time, maybe," Robert said. He saw Nick McKelty approaching, and he knew this was no time for nerd talk. I give him credit for shutting his mouth.

McKelty came lumbering up, his big feet slapping the pavement like clown shoes. He smiled, not in a friendly way, and I could see his after-school snack hanging from the corners of his mouth. It looked like chocolate pudding, or maybe butterscotch.

"Can we hurry up with your little party?" he said. "I've got to get home because my dad is taking me to a private feast at the best Chinese restaurant in Manhattan. In fact, it's the best Chinese restaurant in the world, except for one in China that we're going to this summer."

Of course, we all knew none of this was true. Nick's dad, who owns McKelty's Roll 'N Bowl over on Amsterdam Avenue, was probably buying him a rice bowl at Uncle Ming's Chop Suey House right next door. But Nick McKelty always has to exaggerate everything. We call it the McKelty Factor. Truth times a hundred.

"We just thought we'd show you a little

sample of our secret weapon," Ashley said. "Be afraid, McKelty. Be very afraid."

Ashley gave me the signal, and I took the mound. Frankie got behind home plate and squatted down. He held his mitt out in front of him.

"Put it here, Zip," he hollered.

I reached down and pretended to be scratching my ankle. What I was really doing was making sure the monkey socks were awake and ready to give me some extra luck. I took a deep breath, focused on Frankie's glove, wound up, and released the ball.

Bam! It shot through the air like a cannon, whipping across the plate and landing dead center in Frankie's mitt.

McKelty didn't say a word, but his big jaw flopped open like a barn door in the wind. Ashley smiled at him and waved.

"Just a little sample of what you can expect tomorrow," she said. "Now, if you'll excuse me, we have to get our secret weapon home. We don't want to tire him out."

We walked off the field, leaving McKelty there with his face still flapping in the breeze.

The minute we were off the field, we burst out laughing.

"That was awesome, Zip," Frankie said.

"Yeah, too bad I won't be able to do it tomorrow in the real game," I said, suddenly realizing the awful truth.

"What are you talking about?" Ashley said. "You can and you will."

I shook my head. "Emily will never give me the monkey socks to wear tomorrow. She needs them for the Brain Buster Competition. And, without them, I can't throw worth beans."

"Tell Emily she HAS to let you wear the socks," said Ashley.

"She needs them, too," I answered.

"Actually," Robert said, "your sister is the most brilliant third-grader in the world. You don't need luck when you have a brain like hers." Robert should know. He and Emily are really good friends in a nerdly kind of way.

All the way home, I thought about what Robert had said. Emily didn't need the luck. I did.

The thought rolled around and around in my mind. What if she just couldn't find the monkey socks by tomorrow morning? Things get lost, don't they? It could happen.

Should I or shouldn't I? Should I or shouldn't I? Should I or shouldn't I?

When we got home, I went to my room and took off the white socks. Oh, were my toes happy to be released from the prison of two pairs of tight socks. I could hear Emily outside in the hall, frantically searching every closet in the house for the monkey socks.

Should I or shouldn't I?

Slowly, I peeled off the red monkey socks, tucked them underneath my Mets sweatshirt, and closed the drawer very quietly.

CHAPTER 12

EIGHT REASONS I SHOULD KEEP THE MONKEY SOCKS AND NOT GIVE THEM BACK TO EMILY

1. I have a right to finally win. Don't I?
2. Emily is so smart, she doesn't really need the socks.
3. It really isn't right to keep them, but Emily has to understand I am the one who needs them.
4. It really isn't right.
5. Boy, it really isn't right.
6. Oh, I really want it to be right, but it isn't.
7. Why couldn't it be right?
8. Because it isn't.

CHAPTER 13

OH, DO I HATE BEING GOOD.

Why couldn't I be Nick the Tick? Not only would he have not given his sister the monkey socks, he would have burned them and buried the ashes in the sandbox at school.

I walked around and around my bedroom, making a ring in the carpet from pacing.

I know I should give up the socks, but I can't bring myself to do it.

No matter how closed my door was, I could still hear Emily crying up a storm because her precious little red-and-pink socks were lost.

Wait a minute. Yup, there it is. She's on the hall linoleum pounding her fists and kicking her feet.

Who was she kidding? She couldn't fail if she tried.

Okay! Okay! I can't take it anymore. Here goes nothing.

I flung my door open, ran into the hall, and threw the socks at my sister. One landed right in front of her face and the other fell in the middle of the back of her head, so it looked like she had a third pigtail. Pigtails fit her perfectly. They go so well with her snout for a nose.

I went back in my room and slammed the door. Wow! I didn't know I had so much power. It felt as if the wall shook. My teeth shook.

My mom came running out of the kitchen. "Is everything all right? What's going on?" she asked.

Emily didn't answer.

I didn't answer either. I was in my room walking in that circle again, trying to figure out how I could be so stupid as to give up the socks.

"What were you thinking, Hank?" I kept saying over and over again.

"Henry," my mom called out. "You get out here this instant!"

Maybe one day I will be able to not listen to my name, to not march into the hall and face the firing squad, but today was not that day.

I threw my door open, went into the hall, and I said the shortest sentence I could think of.

"What?" I said, not looking at either of them.

"Don't what me, young man," my mom said. "Where exactly did the socks come from?"

"Well, first they have to pick the cotton to make the material, and then they dye it red. Now once it's out of the dye . . ."

"Henry, cut that out right now," she said in her stern voice. When my mother uses "Henry," no joke in the world can calm her down.

"Okay," I started. "It was a mistake. I wasn't paying attention."

"Big surprise," Emily said.

"Emily, not now," Mom said.

"I wasn't paying attention because I didn't want to keep Papa Pete waiting, Emily. So, I grabbed the first pair of socks on top of the laundry basket. We went to have our catch in the courtyard because I wouldn't be caught dead in those monkey socks in the park. Except they made me pitch better than I ever have before and I really, really need them for tomorrow's game. But, no, Miss I-Do-Everything-Right would never let me borrow them."

"Boy, are you right," Emily interrupted.

"See, what's the use?" I yelled as I ran back into my room and slammed the door again.

A millisecond later, I opened it and screamed from the door jamb. "I think that stinks worse than you stink, Emily Zipzer! And that's that!"

I kicked the door closed. It slammed so hard, it was as if it was shouting to everyone, "Keep out of my room! Keep out of my life! And I really mean it!"

CHAPTER 14

I WAS SO MAD, there was steam coming out of my ears. I flopped down on my bunk bed, put the pillow over my head, and started to scream. I would tell you what I said, but if your parents read those words they would take this book away from you and tell you that you couldn't read it until you were eighteen-and-a-half.

Even through the pillow, I could hear my mom's voice.

"Stan! I need you here."

"I'm busy, Randi," my dad called back. "I found a hair on my earlobe and I'm pulling it out with tweezers."

"That can wait, Stanley."

Oh, no it can't. Dad, keep doing what you're doing.

Apparently, he either got the hair quicker

than he expected or gave up the search for others, because ten seconds later, my dad pushed the door to my room open.

"What's the problem?" he said.

"There's no problem. Emily gets her way, as usual. She's got her monkey socks and I won't be able to pitch for the rest of my life."

"Hank, I have no idea what you're talking about," my dad said.

My mom stuck her head in my room.

"I'm calling a family meeting," she said.

"Why not?" I was still screaming mad. "Let's all sit around and talk about how great Emily is. As a matter of fact, I can't wait. Why don't I just start right now?"

"Calm down, Hank," my dad said. "Let's talk this over like reasonable people."

We sat down at the dining room table. We took the same places we sit in at dinner—my dad at the head, my mom in the one nearest the kitchen, Emily on her left, and me on her right. Or maybe it's me on her right and Emily on her left. Wait a minute, let me figure this out. I know that the pinky finger on my left hand is a little shorter than the one on my right, but I'm on the other side of the table, so I have to stand up and turn my back and then see where the short pinky finger is. Yup, she was on my mom's left.

Emily put Katherine down on the middle of the table.

"Who invited the lizard to our family meeting?" I asked.

Katherine must have known that I was talking about her, because she stared at me with her beady little eyes and then stuck her tongue out at me, as if to say, "I'm here, what do you want to do about it, Zipper Boy?"

"I don't see why we need a family meeting," Emily began. "The creep took my socks. They're my socks, not his socks."

"Hank, your turn to express yourself," said my mom. She believes in expressing yourself.

"I didn't take her socks," I said. "They must have known I needed them and they wound up on my feet. All I'm asking is to wear them for one day and one day only. Not even a day. Just for two hours during the Olympiad softball game. I don't see why that's such a problem."

"Because those are the same two hours that I'm participating in the Brain Buster Competition. And I need my lucky socks to lead the team on to victory."

"What about my victory in the softball game?"

"What victory is that?" Emily the Perfect said. "It would take more than monkey socks to get you to do anything right."

"That's enough, you two," my dad said. "First, let me say that I don't believe monkey socks bring luck."

"Of course," my mom chimed in. "We all know there's no such thing as a lucky charm."

"Although," my dad said, "I do have a silver mechanical pencil, the one I got for being a six-year subscriber to *TIME* magazine. And I do seem to complete my crossword puzzles faster with that particular pencil."

"Stanley, this isn't about your crossword puzzles," my mom pointed out.

"You're right, Randi," he agreed, running his hands through his hair, which was already in its usual messy condition.

"Trust me, Dad," I pleaded. "I need them

more than I've ever needed anything in my whole life."

"Not as much as I need them," said Emily.

My dad held up his hand, letting us both know that we were to stop talking. He looked out at us over the top of his glasses the way he does when he's thinking of an especially hard word in his crossword puzzle.

"Well," he began, "since we're talking about a PAIR of socks, a very clear solution presents itself. There are two children in this family. There are two socks in a pair. We are one family, and one for all and all for one. Are you following my line of thinking?"

"No," I said. "You lost me after 'Well'."

"All right, let me try this," he continued. "Two kids. Two socks. Two divided by two is what?"

"How should I know, Dad?" This conversation was driving me crazy. "Check back with me after sixth grade. Maybe I'll know division by then."

"Two divided by two is one," said Emily. I looked at Katherine, and I know this sounds weird, but she shot me a look as if to say, "Even

I knew that, dodo brain."

I couldn't say this out loud, but I was wondering if I could be dumber than a lizard?

"Stanley, that's a wonderful solution," my mom said. "Each of the children gets one sock."

"It won't work," said Emily the Cheerful.

"Let's put it to a test," said my dad.

My mom was holding the socks that she had scooped up from the hallway where Emily tossed them in her hissy fit. She handed one to each of us. Emily put hers on her left foot. Or maybe it was her right foot. I could do the short pinky finger thing again, but you'd probably stop reading, so let's just say she put it on a foot.

I was a little nervous, because I remembered that last time I put the sock on, her mad-cow iguana attacked my ankle.

"Can you put Katherine in her cage?" I asked Emily.

"And have her miss this?" said Emily.

I rolled my eyes and put the sock on.

"Good," said my dad. "Now let's test this out. Emily, what is your best subject for the Brain Buster Competition?"

"Geography," Emily answered.

"Fine," my dad said. "Emily, name the two longest rivers in the world."

"That's easy," Emily answered. "The Nile and the . . . and the . . . and the . . . I only know one."

"Let's try another question," my dad said. "What is the largest state and what's its capital?"

"The largest state is Alaska. Its capital is . . . is . . . is. I can only answer half the question. See, Daddy, it's because I only have one sock. Hank, give me that sock immediately."

Emily dove for my ankle, but I was quicker than she was. She landed on the carpet, clutching at air.

"Now it's my turn to test out the one sock theory," I said. I grabbed a softball and my glove. "Come on, Dad. Science in action."

We all took the elevator down to the courtyard. Everyone except Katherine. She doesn't like elevators. Once, she freaked out and bit the button for the fifth floor. We had to have my dad pry her off. If you come to my building, you can still see her teethmarks on the button.

When we reached the courtyard, I went to

my place and my dad stood on the metal water drain that we were calling home plate. I did my windup, just like I had done with Papa Pete. The ball left my hand and flew. But, instead of flying into my father's glove, it took off like a wild thing, spun around, and lodged itself in the metal gate that leads to 78th Street.

"Try again," my dad said as he pried the ball loose.

I went through my windup again, and let the ball go. This time, it sailed through the air and was heading for my dad's glove. But then, just before it got there, it took a sudden turn and headed for the clay flowerpot on Mrs. Seides's window ledge. *Bam.* The next thing I knew, the flowerpot was in a million pieces on the courtyard cement.

Mrs. Seides stuck her head out the window.

"I'm so sorry, Mrs. Seides," I said. "I didn't mean to hit your flowerpot, but I couldn't help it, because I only have on one monkey sock."

Mrs. Seides looked confused.

"We'll replace the flowerpot, Miriam," my mom said. "Hank didn't mean to break it."

I turned to my dad.

"You saw it with your own eyes, Dad. Proof that I can't pitch without the socks."

"And I can't remember geography facts without those socks," said Emily.

"Those socks really are lucky," I said.

"I agree," said Emily.

It was the first time ever that my sister and I had agreed on anything.

"Therefore, I NEED the socks," I said.

"I disagree," said Emily.

There we were, disagreeing again. At least we were back to normal.

CHAPTER 15

I SPENT THE HOUR before dinner in my room, trying to figure out how to tell Ashley that I was quitting the team. It's not easy to tell Ashley something she doesn't want to hear. Like if she has a tangerine for lunch and wants to share it with you, and you say, "Tangerines are a little too tangy for me." She won't just say, okay, not everybody likes tangy. She will explain to you why your tongue needs tangy, because it wakes all of your taste buds up so they can appreciate all the tastes that are non-tangy. And the next thing you know, you're eating the tangerine and thinking how lucky you are that Ashley decided to share this wonderful fruit with you.

I took out a piece of paper and wrote this down:

TEN REASONS HANK ZIPZER ABSOLUTELY CANNOT PITCH FOR THE YELLOW TEAM

1. My sister won't let me wear her lucky red-and-pink monkey socks.

I read over what I had written and a bolt of terror shot through me.

That was not a sentence a fourth-grade guy such as myself would want anyone else to see. It gave me the creeps to read it, so think what it would be in the hands of—oh my gosh—I can hardly say it, Nick the Tick McKelty.

Let's say Ashley was walking up the stairs to class. And let's say that the list accidentally fell out of her backpack and Nick McKelty was right behind her to swoop it up in his fingernail-bitten paw. He would run right to Principal Love's office and grab the microphone and read on the public address system to every student at PS 87 that Hank Zipzer wears his sister's red-and-pink monkey socks. Let's say all that happened. Let's say that I would quickly change my name to Bill or even Bernard and get a one-way plane ticket to Alaska and live in an igloo trading whale blubber for the rest of my life.

Wait a minute. I can't do that. They don't have cable in igloos.

I took my list and crumpled it into a ball and threw it in the wastebasket. That wasn't enough. I took it out and shredded it into such small pieces no one could ever tape it back together again.

"Hank, dinner's ready," my mom called. "Come set the table."

I left my room and headed for the dining room.

"It's Emily's night to set," I sulked.

"I set last night," Emily snapped. "It's your turn. Don't you remember? You asked me to switch because you had to study for your Hopi test longer than anyone in the world."

"You two have been at this all afternoon," my mom said. "I've had it. Now, both of you, set the table and no more discussion."

"I'll do the plates and the forks," I said. "No napkins, no knives."

"If I do the napkins and knives, who does the spoons?"

"Hey, mom," I called. "Are we having anything that we have to eat with a spoon tonight?"

"I made carob-soy silk swirl gelati for dessert," my mom said.

"You put out your and Dad's spoon," I said to Emily. "I'll put out Mom's spoon. I won't be needing one. Soy silk isn't my thing."

We were just sitting down to dinner when the doorbell rang.

"I'll get it," Emily and I said at the same time.

"Don't bother," I said to her. "It's not for you."

"How do you know?"

"Because only humans ring doorbells, and what human would want to come visit you?"

"Robert does."

"I rest my case."

I headed for the door. I looked out the peephole and saw Ashley standing there. She was waving a piece of paper around and looking very excited.

I opened the door and she almost fell into the apartment.

"I've got to show you this," she said.

My mom came into the hall. "Hi, Ashley, why don't you stay and have something to eat with us. We're having an all-green dinner—green pasta with raw garden greens."

"Gee, Mrs. Zipzer, you know how I love your dinners. They're so . . . so . . . so . . . unique. But I can't stay. I just came to show Hank this."

"What is it?"

"It's a special edition of the *PS 87 Newsletter*. Listen to this. Headline: 'Ashley Wong First Female Softball Manager in School's History.'"

"Ashley, that's wonderful," my mom said.

"It says that everyone is expecting great things from me. Look, Hank, it even mentions you as our secret weapon."

I couldn't keep it inside anymore.

"Ashley, I can't pitch tomorrow."

"What do you mean? Of course you can pitch. We can't go through this again!"

"Yesterday was a one-time thing. It can't be repeated because a certain someone I know won't share her lucky monkey socks."

"I've decided the only fair thing is that no one wears them," my mom said.

"Mrs. Zipzer, you can't do that," Ashley begged. "You're setting back the cause of women in sports. Look, we're making headlines. Don't you want to see women in the headlines?"

My dad walked out in the hall.

"What's going on here?" he said. "The dinner's getting cold."

"It's supposed to be cold," my mom said. "It's raw."

"Well then, it's getting warm," my dad said.

Boy, our whole family was mighty cranky. Ashley got the message.

"I should go," she said. "Hank, can you meet me in the clubhouse after dinner?"

"I've got math to do."

"How long will it take you?"

"I have to do all the even problems on page 46. Maybe a half hour."

"After homework, then. Seven o'clock. I'll get Frankie."

"What for?"

"You'll see."

CHAPTER 16

WHO WAS I KIDDING? All the even problems on page 46 might take a normal person a half-an-hour, but for me, math is not a get-it-done-quickly subject. I can sit there and look at one problem for a half-an-hour and not have any idea what I'm even supposed to be doing. Except for certain multiplication problems that involve twos, fives, and tens. For some reason, I can multiply anything by those numbers and get the right answer. But show me a seven or a nine and ask me to multiply it by something, and I'm dead meat.

The odd problems looked easier to me. They had a lot of tens and twos in them. Since I was in a rush to get to the clubhouse, I thought it would be a very creative decision to do those instead. I mean, math is math, right?

"I'm going down to the clubhouse for a little

while," I called to my parents.

"Did you finish your math homework?" my mom said.

"I did all eight problems," I said, "and I think I got them right."

In my judgment, she did not need to know that I made the creative decision to do the odd problems. That was between me and me. And me felt like I had the situation under control.

"Okay," my mom said. "You've got thirty minutes. Don't be late."

As I left the apartment, Cheerio jumped off the couch and bolted out into the hall with me. He loves to hang out in our clubhouse. Actually, he loves to hang out anywhere I am, which makes me feel really good.

I pushed B for basement, and the elevator took off on our journey down to the center of the building. Cheerio started to do his circle thing, but I looked at him and said, "Come on, boy. Not tonight. This is a really important meeting, and I need you to act like a regular dog."

Cheerio must have heard in my tone of voice that I meant business, because he stopped chasing his tail and gave me the sweetest little yip you've ever heard. He is my best animal friend, no doubt about it.

When the elevator landed at the basement, Cheerio and I headed down the hall to our clubhouse. We meet in a storage room that has two old couches in the middle, surrounded by shelves full of cardboard boxes with words written on them like WINTER CLOTHES or HOLIDAY DISHES or COLLEGE PHOTOS.

I pushed the door open, but no one was inside. That was strange, because Ashley is never late. Suddenly, a low, creepy voice echoed down the hall.

"Hank Zipzer," the voice said. "You are about to enter the world of spirit. Join the ancient ones."

I whirled around to see where the voice was coming from. The hallway was dark, except for a reddish glow coming from under one of the doors. It was the laundry room door.

I looked down at Cheerio. His eyes were big and round and his ears stood straight up. He tried to yelp, but it sounded more like a yip. If he was human, he'd be saying, "Let's blow this pop stand." Which is exactly what he did. He turned on all four of his little legs and sprang, as much as a dachshund can spring, back into the clubhouse. The last thing I saw was his tail disappearing under one of the couches.

"Hank Zipzer, you are being called to enter the *kiva*!" the voice said. It was starting to get much more familiar.

"Frankie?" I whispered. "Is that you?"

"No," the voice whispered. "It is the eagle spirit come to nest."

"You're nesting in the laundry room?" I said with a laugh.

"The spirits do not appreciate being laughed at," said another voice from inside the laundry room.

"And who are you?" I asked.

"I am the spirit of the owl, bringing wisdom to the night," the voice answered, sounding very much like a certain Ashley Wong.

I pushed the door to the laundry room open, and a blast of steam hit me in the face. Through the mist, I could barely see two figures. They were wearing masks that were decorated with pink feathers and markers. The room was dark, lit only by the red glow of the EXIT sign. As my eyes became more accustomed to the dark, I could see that the steam was rising out of the open tops of the washing machines. The masks the spirits wore were made out of paper plates we use for hot dog lunches.

"Hey, guys, I've only got twenty-five minutes before I have to be back," I said. "What's going on?"

"Then stop fooling around and take your place at the Council Circle," Ashley the Owl said.

I sat down on the floor of the laundry room, and Ashley and Frankie sat on either side of me.

"Wow, it's hot in here," I said. "My T-shirt is starting to stick to me."

"This is our sweat lodge," said Frankie the Eagle.

"It's working," I said, feeling the sweat start to form little lakes behind my knees.

Ashley was holding a wooden cooking spoon with a couple of feathers taped to the end. I was pretty sure I recognized those feathers from a Barbie boa that Ashley used to wear when she pretended to be a rock star.

"I have the talking stick," she said, waving the wooden spoon around. "So I will begin. We are gathered here in our *kiva* to create for you the all-powerful lucky socks you so desire."

She reached into a coffee can that was also decorated with a few pink feathers and pulled out a pair of regular white athletic socks. Ashley handed me the socks, and I saw that she had put red rhinestones in the shape of a monkey face on them. Ashley loves to decorate her clothes, and I mean everything she owns, with rhinestones. She's really good at it, too.

"Wow, Ash, these are great," I said. "You're so artistic. They really look like monkeys. What are they for?"

"For you, dodo brain," she said. "For tomorrow, for the game, for luck. They are the lucky monkey socks you need."

"Thanks so much, guys," I said. "But it takes more than rhinestones to make lucky monkey socks. They have to have been worn by my sister, they have to have been washed first, and they have to have been hidden in the third drawer from the bottom, under my Mets sweatshirt. You can't make socks magic just by putting monkey faces on them."

"I think you're forgetting something, young Hopi brave," said Frankie.

"Shhh," Ashley said to Frankie. "You can't talk. You don't have the talking stick."

"Then pass it over here, Ashweena," said Frankie. "Who said you could hog the talking stick?"

"Guys," I said. "Will someone just take the talking stick, already? I've only got fifteen minutes left."

Ashley picked up the feathered spoon and Frankie grabbed it.

"If the socks aren't lucky enough for you now, we'll fix that," Frankie said. Then he started to chant. "Oh, Spirit of the Ancient Ones, come into the *kiva* and bestow your magic into these monkey socks. Make them lucky for Brave Hank Zipzer."

Frankie waved the socks around.

"Boy, I'm sure glad those socks don't smell," I said.

Ashley shot me a dirty look.

"Come on, Hank. We're doing this for you. Now be serious."

"Okay," I said. I got a really serious look on my face, cleared my throat and shouted, "Animal spirit, show yourself now!"

We waited for something to happen. Now, you're not going to believe this, but the door flung open, and there, standing in our laundry room at 210 W. 78th Street, New York City, was the panting spirit of a small bear.

We of the Council Circle let out an earth-shattering scream and jumped so high, we landed on top of the ancient ceremonial Hotpoint dryer.

CHAPTER 17

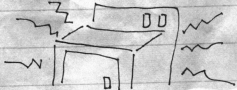

WE WERE CROUCHED on top of the dryer, shivering with fear and excitement. The small bear started to creep toward us, step by step. In the dark, we couldn't see him clearly, but I did see one tuft of brown fur so thick you could stick a spoon in it.

"It's him," Ashley whispered.

"Him who?" I said.

"Your totem spirit," Ashley said. "You asked the Ancient Ones to call him, and he came to fill the lucky socks with his magic."

"Guys," whispered Frankie. "Look."

He pointed to the wall across from us. The red glow from the EXIT sign cast a shadow that made the bear look as if he weighed eight hundred pounds.

"Nice Mister Totem Dude," Frankie said, trying to smile, but I could tell that even he was pretty scared.

"Do you think he's going to do his magic before he eats us?" I said.

"Totem spirits don't eat kids, do they, Hank?" Ashley asked.

"I don't know," I whispered. "They might have left that part out on my tape."

The totem spirit lunged toward us and started to shake.

"Oh, no!" Ashley screamed.

I couldn't help myself. I screamed like a baby, too. Yes, I did. But so did Frankie.

I think we actually scared the bear totem, because he lifted his leg and peed all over those monkey socks.

"Hey, cut that out," Ashley yelled.

"Ashley, you can't talk to the animal spirit like that," Frankie said.

"Spirit, schmirit," she snapped. "There are thirty-five individual rhinestones on each of those socks. Do you have any idea how long that takes?"

Ashley jumped down off the dryer and went toward the bear.

"Back off, buster," she said, wagging her

finger at him. "You don't mess with my rhinestone art."

Frankie and I held our breath and waited to see what would happen. Suddenly, the spirit started to move in a circle. Around and around it went. Was this an ancient Hopi ritual?

As the spirit continued to spin, something very strange began to happen. Its fur started to shift and slide to one side.

Wait a minute. I know that spin.

I looked closely and saw my dog's face poking out from under a furry coat.

"Cheerio?" I yelled.

He stopped spinning, let out a hello yelp, and wagged his tail.

Frankie flipped on the lights. Cheerio was wearing Mrs. Fink's old fur coat that she keeps in a box under the couch in our clubhouse.

As I bent down to pick Cheerio up, I saw the puddle he had left behind. I don't want to gross you out, but the monkey socks were floating in a Cheerio-made lake. We all looked at the socks in silence. Finally, Frankie spoke.

"Maybe," he said, "this sacred liquid gives the socks even more power."

"We'll never know," I said, "because they're not going on any part of my body—no matter how many times you wash them."

"But Zip, the Hopi used all kinds of potions in their magic."

"That's absolutely right," Ashley added. "I think I read that they used antelope poop."

"Good for the Hopi," I said. "But as far as I, Hank Zipzer, am concerned, any magic that was in these socks has been washed away by the Yellow River."

"So what are you going to do tomorrow for the game?" Ashley said.

"I don't know," I answered. "But I do know that if I'm not back in my apartment in three minutes, I'm dead in the water with my mom."

I grabbed Cheerio and took off. Halfway down the hall, it occurred to me that Frankie and Ashley had gone to a lot of trouble to set up that *kiva*. I turned around, ran back to the laundry room, and stuck my head in.

"Thanks, guys," I said. "You tried. Sorry it didn't work out."

"What about me?" Ashley said. "I'm left with only one pitcher. I need backup. What are we going to do tomorrow?"

It was a good question. Unfortunately, I didn't have the answer.

CHAPTER 18

I WAS LYING IN BED THAT NIGHT when the thought came to me like a galloping horse across my brain. We asked for an animal spirit, and Cheerio showed up. Who said totems had to be antelope or snakes or owls or buffalo? Why couldn't they be dachshunds?

I sat up in bed, forgetting about the top bunk, and clunked my head on the board above my bed that holds up the top mattress. But I didn't care, because I had the answer to the question.

Cheerio was my totem spirit, sent to me by the Ancient Ones. I would bring him to my game. He would bring me luck.

I looked around the dark room and saw Cheerio asleep on his pillow next to my bed. He was twitching a little, as if he was dreaming.

I'm sure it was the twitch of a spirit.

CHAPTER 19

"NO WAY," my dad said.

"But, Dad, you don't understand." I was pleading with him. Actually, what I was doing was something between pleading and whining. "I need Cheerio there. He's my lucky charm, my totem. I can't pitch without him."

I was sitting at the kitchen table. Emily had her face in a book, studying last-minute world capitals for the Brain Buster. My dad was at the stove, stirring the oatmeal. He makes us oatmeal for breakfast on special days when he thinks we need extra vitamins and minerals. If ever there was a day I needed extra vitamins and minerals, the day of the Olympiad was certainly it.

"Think about it, Hank," my dad said, putting a steaming bowl of oatmeal down in front of me. "You know Cheerio is high-strung. Now imagine him in your school yard with a crowd of two hundred people. His nerves will kick in and he'll disrupt the entire event."

"He'll behave, Dad."

"Since when? Cheerio does exactly as he pleases. Always has. Always will."

"But, Dad—"

"And even if he does behave, your mother and I are going to be going back and forth between your game and the Brain Buster Competition, which is in the auditorium. They won't let Cheerio in the auditorium."

He had a point there.

"We'll ask for special permission," I said. It was a weak argument, and although I hate to admit it, even I knew it.

"Hank, did you hear what I said? The answer is no. That's N - O."

Oh, boy, he was spelling, and when he spells, it means end of discussion.

"I'm going to get my jacket, kids," my dad said. "Be ready to leave for school in five minutes."

My brain was going a mile a minute as I ate my oatmeal. If I was ever going to get off the bench and touch the ball, I needed a lucky charm. And if I couldn't have the lucky monkey socks, I needed the next best thing. And that was Cheerio. The spirits had spoken, hadn't they? I mean, they had brought Cheerio to our *kiva*. And you don't mess around with stuff that happens in a *kiva*.

I looked around the kitchen, searching desperately for a solution. The refrigerator, the stove, the bulletin board cluttered with notes and takeout menus, the calendar, the spice rack, the phone. The phone!

"Emily, would you mind leaving?"

"Yes," she answered.

I should have known. I had to take it to the next step.

"Emily," I said sweetly. "Katherine was on the windowsill in Mom and Dad's room this morning. Last time I saw her, she was heading down the fire escape."

"You're kidding?" she said.

"Maybe," I said. "But if I were you, I'd check it out for myself. I wouldn't take my word for it."

That worked. She tossed down her book and

105

bolted for our parents' room. I picked up the phone and dialed.

"Hello," Papa Pete answered.

"Hi, Papa Pete," I said. "I've got to talk fast."

"Good," he said. "Then I'll listen fast."

"I need your help," I began. "Can you come here and pick up Cheerio at eleven o'clock and bring him to my school? I want him to see my softball game, but my dad doesn't want to bring him because he's not allowed in the auditorium. But if he stays with you, then he won't have to go into the auditorium, so can you please do this for me?"

"Is it okay with your father?" Papa Pete asked.

"As long as Cheerio behaves, he'll be fine," I said. "Just keep him on the leash."

"I assume you mean Cheerio and not your father," Papa Pete said.

I laughed.

"We'll be there," Papa Pete said. "One tall, proud grandpa. One short, crazy dog."

"I love you, Papa Pete," I said. Which was entirely true.

CHAPTER 20

THE DAY OF THE OLYMPIAD is a big deal at PS 87. Everything is decorated. The cafeteria has streamers, the bulletin boards have signs that say GO BLUE or YELLOW RULES. Even the trash cans are wrapped in crepe paper. Usually, they're green, which is our school color. But on Olympiad Day, half of them are blue and the other half of them are, you guessed it, yellow.

When we walked up to school, Principal Love was waiting outside. Talk about school spirit, he was overflowing with it. I'm not kidding—even his clothes were cheering. For starters, he was wearing a scarf that his wife had knit that was half yellow and half blue. I noticed that the yellow half was hanging down the front of his overcoat, and the blue half was in the back. I wondered if that meant he was a yellow-ie at heart.

"Check out the feet," Frankie whispered.

Principal Love always wears black Velcro shoes that squeak when he walks up and down the linoleum halls. On this particular day, he had replaced those beauties with two other Velcro shoes. One was blue. And the other was, you guessed it, yellow.

"Where do you even buy shoes like that?" I whispered to Frankie and Ashley.

"A clown store?" Frankie suggested.

"No, silly, they're homemade," said Ashley. "I bet he got white shoes and colored them with magic markers."

"I hope it doesn't rain," Frankie said. "He'll end up with polka-dot shoes."

"Good morning, students," Principal Love said in his loudspeaker voice. "Welcome to the Olympiad."

"Hi, Principal Love," we all muttered.

"Remember, children, the body, the mind, and the spirit all win today—regardless of whether you actually win or not. There's no losing in winning and no losing in losing. Isn't that right, Mr. Zipzer?"

"Absolutely, Principal Love," I said, even

though I had no idea of what he had just said. Everything he says sounds like it belongs in some really important library book. I'm sure as soon as someone figures out what he's talking about, they're going to write it down.

"And what team are you participating in today, Mr. Zipzer?" he asked.

I didn't answer, but Ashley jumped right in.

"He's pitching for the Yellow Softball Team," she said right into his face. "And I'm not sure whether you know this or not, Principal Love, but I am the first female softball team manager in the history of PS 87."

"Of course I know that, Manager Wong," he said. "I read my newsletter cover to cover. I believe it's a new age for women and that their particular age makes no difference in this age."

Wow, he was doing it again. I think that sentence is going in the same book. Maybe he'll call it *Long Sentences That Make No Sense At All* by Leland Love. I'd use my library card to check that one out.

As we were going up the stairs, Nick McKelty was racing down them. He was already wearing his blue T-shirt and carrying the bases to set up the softball diamond.

"Hey, Yellow Team punks," he said. "I don't know why you guys even bothered to show up today. You got no chance of winning. We're going to wipe the bases with you."

"Yeah, and my name is Bernice," Frankie said.

No matter how many times I hear Frankie say that, it always makes me smile.

"And my name is Bruce," McKelty shot back and laughed his hyena laugh as though he had said something funny. His comeback was so un-funny that we couldn't even come back with a comeback.

"Gotcha!" McKelty said, and flicked me under the chin. "And good luck with your little throwing arm today. Hope it doesn't give out on you."

When we hit the second floor, Mr. Rock passed by us in the hall. He's the music teacher and a really cool guy. In fact, he's the teacher who first suggested to me that maybe I have dyslexia. And he didn't make me feel bad when he said it.

"Hey, kids," he said. "Hurry to your classroom and pick up your T-shirts. You should warm up before the game. Ashley, are you ready with your starting lineup?"

"Pretty much," Ashley answered, "except for Hank. He's giving me a hard time about pitching."

"You kids go on ahead," Mr. Rock said to Ashley and Frankie. "Let me have a word with Hank."

I tried to avoid his eyes. When Mr. Rock looks at you, you're forced to tell the truth.

"So, what's up?" he said. "Are you having last-minute jitters?"

"First, last, and in-between minute jitters," I said. "I can't pitch. Everyone knows that."

"Ashley thinks you can. Frankie, too. They told me you're the team's secret weapon. They say you've got a mean fast pitch."

"I only threw that pitch for one day. Then it disappeared. I don't know where it came from. I don't know where it went."

"It's in there somewhere," Mr. Rock said, pointing to my middle section. "If you did it once, you can do it again. Just concentrate on what you're doing."

"That only works for most people," I said. "Not for me."

Suddenly, it smelled like there was an open can of old tuna fish next to us. Mr. Rock must have smelled it, too, because we both turned our heads at the same time. Yup, there he was. Nick McKelty, the mouth breather, letting out gobs of bad breath. I looked down and the fabric of my shirt was starting to wrinkle.

"A little pre-game chatter?" he said, shooting some of his fishy breath over my way.

"Mr. McKelty, isn't there some place you need to be?" Mr. Rock said.

"Yeah, the pitcher's mound." Nick the Tick grinned. "I'm gonna have the Yellow Team for lunch." He gave me a slap on the back with his paw-sized hand. "This little guy is my first course."

McKelty galloped off down the hall. I looked at Mr. Rock.

"What's the use?" I said. "I was born to be on the bench."

"Hank, you've got a decision to make, and today's the day. Do you really want to sit on the sidelines your whole life? Or are you going to get in the game?"

Mr. Rock didn't say another word. He just turned and walked away.

Life is filled with questions, isn't it? Whoa, do I wish I had a few answers.

CHAPTER 21

HOW DID I GET HERE? On the mound. I'm sure I said no over and over again to Ashley and Frankie and to anyone who would listen. But here I am, with two hundred people looking at me. Every eye on me. Every person waiting for me to do something. Anything.

Principal Love stood next to the bleachers, tapping his Velcro sneakers on the artificial turf, staring at me.

It was exactly noon. We had been playing for almost an hour, and the score was 6 to 5 in favor of the Yellow Team. It was the last inning, and the Blue Team was up. There was still time for them to score and win the game.

My Yellow Team had used four pitchers, and for one reason or another, they all had to leave the game. Even our ace, Ryan Shimozato, who had pitched every one of his Little League games since first grade without so much as a sprained ankle, had to leave the field. Normally, Ryan's a ball-throwing machine, but, wouldn't you know it, in the last inning of the Olympiad game, he trips over second base on his way to third and lands on his right hand. His pitching hand.

I had been sitting on the bench the whole game. Actually, I had been sitting on my mitt with the ball in it, which is not all that comfortable. Papa Pete hadn't shown up with Cheerio. My confidence level was so low, it felt like it was around my ankles.

When I saw Ryan catch his left foot under the second base bag, my heart sank. He flew through the air as if in slow motion, bounced on his right side, and, yup, landed on his right pitching hand.

Everyone in the stands was up on their feet. Only one person on that whole entire field was high-fiving the rest of his teammates. You know who that was . . . of course you do. It was Nicky Ticky McKelty.

"Alright!" the big moron yelled. "They lost another pitcher! The Blue Team rules!"

Ms. Adolf, who was umping the game, ran as best as she could to see if Ryan was okay. I could tell he was trying not to cry in front of that big crowd. I know how that feels. I started yelling, "Way to go, Ryan! You are the coolest!"

Ashley tried to put me in to pitch for Ryan, but I refused. I was waiting for Cheerio before I'd step out on that field. So she put Heather Payne in. Heather managed to strike Sasha Nabakov out, which wasn't that hard because Sasha just moved here from Russia and they don't even have softball there. Then Heather threw a big, fat, slow ball to Hector Ruiz and he hit a double. Ashley called a time-out.

She and Frankie came running up to me. I was on the bench behind the chain-link fence, and with Ashley and Frankie on the other side, I felt like I was in a television show about prison where I was the prisoner and they were my visitors.

"Hank, we need you," Ash said.

"No, you don't," I answered.

"Yes, we do," added Frankie. "It's the last inning. We only have one out. The tying run is on. Heather can't pitch her way out of a paper bag. We need you to pitch, Zip, or we could lose this game."

"You think you need me, but your thoughts are kablooey," I said.

"Hank, we're out of pitchers," Ashley pleaded. "Come on!!! You can do this. As manager, I know these things. You've done this before, Hank."

Yeah, in the empty courtyard of our building.

"Hey, Frankie, you do it," I said, as if I had just come up with a great idea.

"I'm catching," Frankie said. "Hank, breathe. And I'm talking really deep. All you have to do is just listen to the sound of my voice."

"Hey, guys, turn around," I said to Ashley and Frankie.

They did and saw what I saw. The entire crowd was leaning forward, trying to hear what was going on.

"Hank, you can do this. Correction. You *have* to do it. Just keep your eyes on where you want the ball to go," Frankie said, getting in my face. "It's you and me. We can do this."

"I'm so scared," I whispered. "I can't stop my hands from shaking."

I put my hands in my pockets so no one would notice them quivering. I looked out in the stands, hoping desperately that Papa Pete had arrived with Cheerio. He hadn't, but I did see my mom and dad walking out onto the field. Emily was with them, and she was looking very happy. She probably knocked them dead in the Brain Buster. And here I was, too scared to even go out on the field.

All of a sudden, Nick the Tick started yelling at me from the Blue Team bench.

"Pitcher has a bellyache. Pitcher has a headache. Pitcher is a wimp." His team started laughing really hard. Ms. Adolf left her place behind home plate and headed straight for us. I'm not trying to be rude, but you've got to see Ms. Adolf in her umpire's outfit. She looked prehistoric. With her face mask and chest plate and leg guards that went from her knees to her ankles, she looked like a very angry brontosaurus. The shin guards made her walk stiff-legged, so she kicked up a cloud of dust as she moved toward us.

"Oh, no. This is just what I need now," I said to Ashley, who turned around just in time to see the Adolfosaurus looming large above her.

"Manager Wong, what seems to be the problem?" Ms. Adolf snarled.

"I'm just making a decision about who's going in to pitch," Ashley said, trying to sound casual.

"If you don't make a decision right away, and I mean in fifteen seconds, the Blue Team will win by default. Am I clear?" Ms. Adolf said.

"Ms. Adolf, we truly need Hank on the mound, but he's afraid he will make a fool of himself," Frankie explained.

"Just concentrate," Ms. Adolf told me. "Keep your eye on where you want the ball to go."

"That's exactly what Frankie told him," Ashley said exactly.

"We're talking word for word," Frankie said.

Oh, great, just great. Let me see if I've got this right. My parents are both here with my smarty pants younger sister. Nick the Tick is yelling at me and his Blue Team is falling all over themselves, laughing at me. Ms. Adolf has given me fifteen seconds to walk out to the mound and embarrass myself for as long as I live or lose the game for my team. And I feel . . . what do I feel?

I feel the need to throw up.

CHAPTER 22

"HANK, IT'S NOW OR NEVER," I said to myself.

Go, feet. Walk out onto the field. On your mark. Get set. Go.

"Okay, Frankie. It's you and me."

I did it. I walked onto the field without saying another word. I did not look to the right or left. I did not even look at my parents. As I made my way to the pitcher's mound, all of a sudden, out of nowhere, I heard a full orchestra playing marching music in my head.

"Concentrate, Hank," I kept repeating over and over. I turned around to face home plate. Frankie was right where he was supposed to be, kneeling down in the catcher's position.

And then there was silence!

I'm not kidding. If the crowd was yelling, if

McKelty was screaming his big thick head off, I couldn't hear any of them.

Frankie looked at me through the protective bars of his catcher's mask. Man, was he intense. It felt as if there was a thread connecting his eyes with my eyes.

As if in slow motion, he nodded his head up and down. I knew what he was saying to me, too. "You can do this, Hank. Keep your eye on my mitt. Let's go, Zip Man." He said all that with just a nod.

It was one out and we were ahead by one run. Hector Ruiz was on second base and Katie Sperling was up at bat.

The most beautiful girl in our class, or at least in the top two, is standing at the plate with her long red hair blowing in the slight breeze, the bat just off her shoulder. She is staring at me . . . waiting.

"Pitch the ball, Hank!" I screamed silently to myself.

Frankie's eyes were screaming the same thing.

I put my feet on the mound, which was really a strip of rubber just big enough for your sneaker. I started to wind up. First, I twisted my upper body around so it was facing second base, while my lower body faced home plate. Then I stuck out my left leg. No . . . right. I bent at the waist so my head was pointing toward third base. The whole time, my right hand was holding the ball that was resting in the palm of my mitt. Then, I stretched both arms toward first base, raised them over my head as high as I could, and let the ball go—underhand—toward Frankie's mitt.

There it was—my pitch.

I call that sweet throw the Zippity Zinger and, as a matter of fact, that name just popped into my head.

I'm sure my technique must have looked a little strange, because everyone in the crowd seemed to be staring at me with their mouths open.

The ball flew through the space between me and Katie and, *whop!* It sailed past her and into Frankie's mitt.

"Strike one!" Ms. Adolf yelled as her hand shot out from her side to make the strike sign.

Before she put the bat back in the ready

position, Katie looked at me and cocked her head as if to say, "Hank, come on . . . it's me, Katie."

Frankie knows I can't really catch well, so he threw the ball back to me short so it would hit the ground and roll the rest of the way. I scooped up the ball in my mitt and got ready for another Zippity Zinger. I let the ball go the same way as before, only this time Katie connected with the ball and it came straight at me.

I panicked. I can't catch, remember? I didn't want to let the other team score, so I turned my body to the right and stopped the ball with my left side. My entire left side. Oh, wow, oh, wowie, did that hurt.

I'm going to have a humongous black-and-blue mark on the old rib cage later. I can't think about that now.

The ball hit me and dropped to the ground. I picked it up and threw it to the first baseman, who caught it and tagged the base. Ms. Adolf called Katie Sperling, "Out!"

Katie returned to her bench without looking back at me. Her team greeted her with, "Way to go, Katie. Good try, kid." Nick McKelty's big ham of a hand slapped her on the back and she almost fell face first onto the bench.

Two outs and only one more to go.

Oh, no. McKelty is up.

On his way to the batter's box, Nick the Tick picked up every bat leaning against the fence. Finally, he decided on the one he calls the Aluminum Beauty.

As he walked up to the plate, he never took his eyes off me. And he didn't stop talking either.

"Hey, Zipper Head, you going to stop my ball with your head? Hey, Zippy, you pitch like a mouse. Alright. Give me what you got. Oh, right, that would be nothing."

"Nicholas, remember to practice sportsmanship," Ms. Adolf reminded him. Like that big jerk had ever heard of the word.

Just before McKelty went into his stance, he pointed his bat toward the outfield.

"That's where I'm going to hit the ball," he shouted. Principal Love thought that was just great. He smiled as McKelty shoved his bat in the air toward Amsterdam Avenue, which was just beyond the fence.

Cheerio! Where are you? I need you, boy. I need a lucky charm. I can't do this alone.

I could feel myself starting to fall apart. I blinked my eyes. They were starting to get blurry.

Come on, Papa Pete. Where are you? Please, please, please show up with Cheerio.

When I opened my eyes, I saw a dust cloud moving along under the bleachers. A tiny tornado was making its way under the second row. Everyone sitting in that row started waving their arms to clear the air.

Wait a minute. Can that be? Is that Papa Pete on his hands and knees, chasing after the cloud?

Fortunately and unfortunately, the answer to that question was yes. I had gotten my wish, alright. Papa Pete did show up with Cheerio. But Cheerio had broken free of his leash, and Papa Pete was trying to grab him as he spun his way along the bleachers to the field. Every time Papa Pete reached for Cheerio, my nutty little dog would yip and twirl away from him like an out-of-control ballerina. Cheerio, my little dust devil, was making his way to the batter's box. And rather quickly, I might add.

McKelty jumped out of the way just in time to avoid Cheerio, but Ms. Adolf wasn't so quick. Cheerio spun out onto the field, doing his crazy circle dance around her. She tried to step out of his way, but she couldn't move too well with all her umpire gear on. Cheerio lodged himself somewhere between her right foot and her left foot, and kept spinning. Ms. Adolf went down like a sack of potatoes. She sprawled on the dust like a brontosaurus trapped in a tar pit. And the cherry on top was Papa Pete crawling like a gigantic version of a land crab, trying to grab Cheerio's leash just before that hot dog took off again.

I couldn't believe my eyes. One thing I did know, however:

My life as I knew it was now officially over. So much for the Hopi totem spirits.

CHAPTER 23

IT TOOK A FEW MINUTES to catch Cheerio. My mom and dad ran out on the field, and Emily, too, but Cheerio kept escaping when they tried to grab him. It was Papa Pete who finally captured him by tossing his red warm-up jacket over him and scooping him up in his arms. Poor Cheerio. He looked like a shiny, red banana. Everyone in the crowd was laughing, and when my little dog poked his face out of the jacket, he looked scared.

"That's okay, fella," Papa Pete said to him in a really gentle voice. "Let's wave to the nice people out there."

Papa Pete held up one of Cheerio's paws and waved it toward the bleachers. Everyone cheered, and I could see Cheerio's tail start to wag underneath the jacket. I was glad he wasn't scared anymore.

Luckily, Ms. Adolf wasn't hurt. I guess all that brontosaurus gear protected her. She was pretty messy, though, and my mom and dad helped her brush all the dirt off. While they were cleaning her up, Frankie and Ashley took the opportunity to come to the pitcher's mound to see how I was doing.

"Well, there's your powerful animal spirit," Frankie said, pointing at Cheerio, who was snuggled up in Papa Pete's arms.

I didn't answer Frankie.

"Zip," Frankie said louder, snapping his fingers in front of my eyes. "Over here. Look at me. We have a game to win, remember?"

"What do I do now?" I wanted to know. "I can't concentrate on the game."

"Listen to me, Zippola," Frankie said in his no nonsense voice. "Forget the socks. Forget Cheerio. Just concentrate on my glove and throw the ball."

"Do the pitch we know you can do," said Ashley.

"You mean the Zippity Zinger?" I said. "I think I may have a couple of those left."

"See, that's what I'm talking about," Frankie

said. "That's the spirit, Hank."

"And we mean that in the Hopi way," Ashley said. She smiled a real smile at me. I have to admit, I have great friends.

"Play ball!" the Adolfosaurus shouted from behind home plate.

McKelty stepped back into the batter's box.

"What's the matter?" he shouted. I thought I could smell his bad breath all the way on the pitcher's mound. "Pitcher's got a bellyache? Come on, Zipper Head. I can't wait to win."

"Concentrate, Hank," I said under my breath.

My parents were in the stands now. They had looked pretty upset at first, but now they were concentrating on me and the game. Cheerio was asleep in Papa Pete's jacket, and Emily had her hand on his back. She smiled at me, and mouthed the words, "Good luck." That's right, you read it correctly. Emily Grace Zipzer smiled and wished me good luck. You know, when times are tough, it's kind of nice to have a sister.

I checked on Hector Ruiz on second. He had been standing there for so long, his legs must have been really tired.

Now, down to business.

Frankie got into his catcher's crouch. He pointed at me and then pointed back to himself. I nodded. As if by magic, the sound of the crowd started to drift away again. And I wound up to let loose a Zippity Zinger.

My body turned this way and my legs stretched that way. My hands flew out toward first base, then like an arrow, shot right into the sky, and the ball became an eagle that flew right past Nick the Tick's bat before he took his first swing.

"Strike one!" Ms. Adolf shouted and made her strike sign.

Can it be true? Did I just do that?

Frankie stood up and ripped the mask off his face. He did not say a word. He didn't have to. He put the mask on and threw the ball back to me so it would roll the last few feet to my glove.

This time, my body started the pitch, but I felt different. I started to relax and just let my arms and legs and waist and hand flow through their motions.

Wham!

The ball left my fingertips and McKelty was really concentrating on it. His eyes were like laser beams trying to bring the ball to his bat. He swung his Aluminum Beauty and hit the ball hard, but it shot backwards. It was going for Ms. Adolf, but just before it reached her, she dropped to her knees into the dirt and it sailed into the chain-link fence behind her.

Wow! Maybe Ms. Adolf was a professional ballplayer before she became a teacher. She falls just like they do during a TV game.

Ms. Adolf got up, brushed herself off, and used the same brush to dust off home plate.

"Strike two!" she shouted.

This time, Frankie threw the ball back directly to my mitt . . . and I caught it!

I quickly turned to Papa Pete, whose smile was so big that I could see all his teeth from under his black mustache. I could feel his love all the way out on the mound.

Two strikes, two outs. Hector Ruiz leading off, just itching to race toward home plate. McKelty ready to hit the winning run.

Let me tell you, this is a dream I never ever thought I would be in. Wait a minute, it's not over yet. It could become a nightmare in one pitch.

I twisted to second and stuck my leg out like I was an ostrich. At that moment, with my head pointing to third, I lost focus. When I let go of the ball this time, it didn't sail. It wobbled and hit the ground, rolling past McKelty's feet as if there were ten bowling pins behind home plate.

"Ball one!" Ms. Adolf yelled.

"Hey, Zitface, this isn't bowling," McKelty shouted. "The game's called softball, remember? Oh, right, you can't remember stuff."

Ashley yelled from the bench. "Bring it back, Hank! Don't listen to that boob! Come on now! We need strikes! Throw strikes."

I looked at Frankie and leaned toward him a little. I don't know why I did that, but all the Mets pitchers do it so I thought I would try it.

He pointed at the center of his mitt and then hit it three times really hard. He was telling me to put the ball "right there." But could I do it again? All I needed was one more strike. Could I throw another Zippity Zinger?

"Hey, Zipper—you can't do anything right, so why try?" McKelty shouted. "Just put it over the plate and I'll put the ball over the fence to finish the game."

I took a moment to regroup. Ms. Adolf got her head in position to see where the ball was going. Frankie was statue-still, his mitt in front of him making a perfect target. The entire crowd knew how important this pitch was. My parents; Frankie's parents, the Townsends; Ashley's parents, Dr. and Dr. Wong; Mr. Rock and Dr. Lynn were all standing, waiting.

I looked at my mom and dad, Papa Pete and Emily. Every fear I ever had came rushing in and filled my brain.

Now or never, Hank. What's it going to be? Just pitch like you have been. "Easy for you to say," I told myself.

My upper body twisted to second base, my leg started to lift itself off the ground as if it was floating. My head pointed toward third and, this time, I did not leave any part of the Zippity Zinger out. I kept my eyes on the center of Frankie's mitt and let the ball roll off my fingertips.

McKelty's bat started its rotation from his shoulder all the way around his body, and he hit that ball hard. So hard I felt sorry for the ball.

Thwack! was the sound on contact and it rang in my ears.

Everything happened in slow motion after that.

Frankie ripped off his mask, never taking his eyes off the ball. All the heads in the crowd looked up at the ball in flight. Ms. Adolf lifted off her mask and stared up into the sky. Ashley pressed her face up against the fence. My mother was clamped onto my father's arm, their eyes glued to that ball.

The entire Yellow Team on the field watched that ball, shielding their eyes with their gloves. The Blue Team on their bench jumped forward and pressed their fingers through the fence to see where the ball would land.

The ball . . . instead of heading toward the left field fence, had sailed straight up and was falling toward Earth, right over my head.

One thing I know for sure is that I can't catch under pressure. So I darted off the pitcher's mound and moved toward first base to clear the way for Frankie. He came running from home plate just in time to catch the ball. In a single movement, we both spun around to Nick McKelty and yelled in one voice, "You're out!"

The only thing Ms. Adolf could do was yank her thumb in the air, which was her sign for "you're out!" McKelty looked at her in disbelief.

Oh, yeah!

I had made Nick the Tick hit a pop fly and that fact made me fall down in excitement, pride, and disbelief.

Everyone on the Yellow Team came running up and jumped on me, yelling and screaming. I was on the bottom of the pile with just my head sticking out. Ashley was lying down on the ground in front of me. Her glasses were crooked and her baseball cap was on sideways.

"Hank, you did it! You did it! I'm so proud of you!" she laughed.

"Hey, I can't breathe down here," I tried to yell.

One by one, the kids got off the pile. I imagined that by the time they were all off, I would be flatter than a pancake—for real.

Frankie helped get the kids off and then lifted me back to my feet.

This is what good pals we are. He did not have to say a word to me. He looked me in the eye and I knew every thought he had and I felt the same way.

I was really glad to be his friend, too.

CHAPTER 24

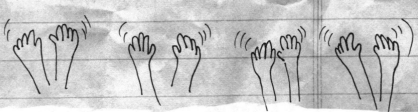

WE SAT ON THE STAGE of the auditorium, the Blue Team on the left and the Yellow Team on the right. All the parents and guests were in the audience, and the teachers were lining the walls. Everyone was waiting for the same thing—to find out which team won the Olympiad.

Principal Love was going on about how competition was good for the growth of character. I was too excited to listen to him. All I wanted to know was if the Yellow Team was going to win so I could get that medal around my neck. I know you're not supposed to care about winning and losing, but when there's a gold medal involved, I don't see how that's possible. Who doesn't want a medal? Nobody I know.

"I'm keeping my fingers crossed," I whispered to Frankie. And was I ever. In fact, my fingers were turning blue from being crossed so tight.

"And so," Principal Love was saying, "our competition today is part of a chain that can be traced all the way back to the roots of competition, when human beings first realized that competing was the very nature of competition."

If they gave a gold medal for sentences that clog up your brain because you can't figure them out, I think Principal Love would have a neck full of them.

"And now for the results of today's Olympiad," he said.

"Finally," Ashley whispered to me. She had put on a white baseball cap that said GIRL MANAGERS RULE in yellow rhinestones.

"No matter what happens, you made history today," I said to her.

"You made it into the record books yourself," she said with a smile. "The first ever Zippity Zinger. No one will ever be able to do it again."

"Including me," I said.

"That's for sure," said Frankie, "or my name isn't Bernice."

"Frankie, your name isn't Bernice." I said. And all three of us laughed.

"I'd like to call to the stage our faculty coaches," Principal Love said. "Mr. Michael Sicilian for the Blue Team." Everyone on the Blue Team applauded like crazy. "And for the Yellow Team, Ms. Fanny Adolf."

Frankie, Ashley, and I looked at one another and our mouths fell open.

"Fanny?" we all said at once.

"As in rear end?" Ashley said.

"As in tush?" I said.

"Ms. Buttocks Adolf," said Frankie. "That is too funny to be true."

Ashley started singing in a tiny whisper. "Fanny, Fanny Bo Banny, Banana Fanna Fo Fanny, Me My Mo Manny, Fanny."

We tried not to laugh, and trust me, we were not the only kids in that auditorium trying not to laugh.

I looked out in the audience and saw my parents. My mom was giving me the Look. You know the one. It's that same look you get if your aunt farts at the dinner table and, even though it's the funniest thing you've ever heard,

140

you have to pretend it didn't happen.

"We've tabulated the scores," Principal Love said. "As we all know, the Blue Team, led by Emily Zipzer, won the Brain Buster part of the Olympiad, earning one hundred points."

I looked over at Emily. She looked so happy. I was really glad for her. Honestly and truly. I glanced at Robert, who was sitting with our team, and he had the same grin on his face that Cheerio gets after we give him a biscuit.

"In the Softball Competition," Principal Love continued, "the victory goes to the Yellow Team, earning them one hundred points. A special hats off goes to the Yellow Team's secret weapon, Hank Zipzer."

Everyone in the auditorium started to applaud. I thought my ears were going to drop right off my head. It was the best sound I had ever heard. I never thought I would be able to do what I did today, and here was a room full of people applauding for me. I looked around the room at the people clapping, and mostly it was a blur. But I did see Dr. Lynn and Mr. Rock, who were both smiling directly at me and clapping really hard. My parents looked so proud, and Papa Pete actually got out of his chair and raised his fist in a victory salute.

"Hankie," he yelled in his big voice. "Atta boy!"

I felt Frankie's elbow in my ribs.

"Zip, look over there."

He pointed over to the center of the stage, where Ms. Adolf was standing next to Principal Love. She was clapping, too. I repeat. Ms. Fanny Adolf was clapping for me.

And they say miracles never happen.

CHAPTER 25

By the way, did I mention that the Yellow Team won the Olympiad and that I'm now wearing a gold medal around my neck?

Well, we did. And I am.

It was a tight race for us, though. The deciding factor was the Triple C event, the Clean and Clutter-Free Competition. Our team scored really well on that, thanks to Robert. In the Clean Desk category, he blew the judges away by bringing in a mini-vac and sucking up all those little pencil shavings that fall out of the pencil sharpener and collect in the corners of your desk. We got bonus points for that.

That Robert, he does come in handy sometimes.

You won't believe what lost it for the Blue Team. Picture this. The judges are at the Blue Team's desks and they come to Luke

Whitman's. While they're checking his desk to see if it's orderly and uncluttered, he reaches into his back pocket where he keeps a half of peanut butter and jelly sandwich because he never wants to be without a snack. Luke had to sneeze and couldn't find a tissue, so he took his sandwich out, unwrapped it, and get this, blew his nose in wax paper.

If that wasn't bad enough, when he took the wax paper away from his honker, there was a mixture of chunky peanut butter and boogers spread like silly putty across his face.

If you're going to lose a Clean and Clutter-Free Competition, that's the way to do it. If it were up to me, I would have given Old Luke extra points for grossness, but the judging committee didn't see it that way. Which I guess is good, because in case I didn't mention it before, I am wearing a Yellow Team gold medal around my neck.

CHAPTER 26

AFTER THE MEDAL PRESENTATIONS, Papa Pete offered to take everyone out for a celebration. We walked over to McKelty's Roll 'N Bowl, where Papa Pete is a regular at the coffee shop. We were a big group—Frankie and his parents, Ashley and her parents, Robert and his mom, Emily and me and our parents, Papa Pete, and, of course, Cheerio.

Papa Pete ordered root-beer floats for everyone except Cheerio. He had his favorite—an order of chili fries. Light on the chili, though, because it gives him gas. Believe me, you don't want to be around Cheerio when he's got gas.

Papa Pete made a toast to all the kids, not just for winning, but for participating in the Olympiad. Then I clinked my spoon on my glass to get everyone's attention, and stood up.

"I want to thank the two best friends any

winning pitcher could have," I began. "First of all, my manager, Ashley, who wouldn't take no for an answer." I turned to Ashley. "Ash, I don't know how you knew that I could do this, but because you did, I feel better than I've ever felt in my whole life."

"Better than when we got that stink bomb and threw it down the elevator shaft while Mrs. Fink was in the elevator?"

"Ashley," I whispered. "What are you, nuts?"

I turned to my mom and tried really hard to laugh. "That Ashley," I said. "She has such a wacky imagination."

My mom gave me another one of her "we need to talk about this" looks. I thought I had better go on with my speech really quickly, before there was time for any questions from the parent section.

"Frankie, you are the man," I said. "It's amazing how you talked me through that last inning. Without you, I would never have been able to do what Ashley knew I could do but I thought I couldn't do."

"Zip, if I understood one word of what you

just said, I think I would be deeply touched," said Frankie.

Everyone at the table laughed.

"To the good Doctors Wong, and to Dr. and Mrs. Townsend, and to Mrs. Upchurch, thank you for having great kids," I went on. "And to Papa Pete, who has been playing catch with me for as long as I can remember, I'd like to make you the honorary inventor of the Zippity Zinger."

"Hankie," said Papa Pete, wiping some whipped cream off his mustache. "Of all my inventions, and that includes the Knockwurst with Baked Beans and Sauerkraut on Corn Rye with Only Yellow Mustard Special Sandwich, the Zippity Zinger is the one I'm most proud of."

I looked over at my sister. She was sitting next to Robert. Don't gag or anything, but they were holding hands.

"Emily, none of this would have happened without your lucky monkey socks, so thank you for having them in the first place. And congratulations on winning the Brain Buster. I really do appreciate how smart you are, especially since it takes a lot of pressure off me. At least Mom and Dad got one smart kid."

Emily reached over to try to give me a hug, but, fortunately, I was quick enough to avoid her arms. Wrapping herself around me was not necessary. Plus, it was completely unacceptable in a crowd.

"And, last but not least, I want to thank my mom and dad for showing me that you don't need a lucky charm to launch a Zippity Zinger."

My mom smiled and blew me a kiss, which I'd rather she wouldn't do in public, but I've learned that there's no stopping her. My dad took the pencil out from behind his ear and waved it at me. That was big because unless he's going to write a word down or across, his pencil lives behind his ear full-time.

Suddenly, I felt a hot wind on my neck. Then I smelled onions burned in a tar pit. I turned around and looked directly into the mouth of Nick McKelty. His teeth headed in every direction—north, south, east, west—except up and down. He was laughing like a hyena.

"The Zippity Zinger, that's a laugh," he

said, spraying small drops of saliva on my chin. "There's no such thing. You're just one lucky little dude."

"You're right, McKelty," I said. "I am lucky. And I am little. But guess what, big guy? I won."

I held up the gold medal. The reflection from the disco ball caught it and a ray of golden light flickered on McKelty's face.

"Nick, I'll bet yours looks great in the light, too," Ashley said.

"Oh, I'm so sorry," I said. "You don't have a medal. What a shame."

"Hey, there's always next year when you repeat fourth grade," Frankie added.

I picked up my root-beer float and clinked glasses with Frankie and Ashley. McKelty stomped away to where his father was waiting for him at the shoe counter. The last thing I saw before I turned back to the table was him spraying foot deodorant into a pair of size nine red-and-tan bowling shoes.

He does that so well. There's a future for everybody.

"This calls for a toast," I said. I raised my

glass high in the air. Unfortunately, I raised it too high. Way too high.

The thing I'd like to mention here about root beer with ice cream floating in it is that when you fling it in the air, it sails out of the glass, goes straight up, and lands with a big plop on the front of your pants—in the immediate area of your zipper.

When I looked at the root beer spreading like a wild river across my pants, it looked like one thing and one thing only. I am sorry and embarrassed to have to bring this up, but the truth is, it looked like I had peed in my pants.

If I had thought my mom blowing me a kiss in public was embarrassing, you can imagine how I felt when I saw her hands moving toward me with a napkin.

"Mom," I shouted. "Stop right there. Think about what you're doing!"

She froze. I froze. My zipper froze.

Man, that ice cream was cold.

CHAPTER 27

EXIT

TEN WAYS TO GET OUT OF A BOWLING ALLEY WITHOUT PEOPLE NOTICING YOU HAVE A ROOT-BEER FLOAT RUNNING DOWN YOUR PANTS

1. Put your hands over your stomach, double over, pretend you're about to throw up, and run out.
2. Drop to the floor as if you're looking for a quarter that fell out of your pocket and crawl to the front door.
3. Take your friends' drinks and pour them on you, too, and then tell everyone you're going to a costume party as a root-beer float.
4. Pull your shirt out of your pants, pull it down over your knees, and hop out of the room like a rabbit.
5. Bowl yourself out of there. Get a running

start, dive belly-first onto the oil-slick lane, put your hands in front of you, and head for the ten pin. Exit on the other side of the pins. This is a little dangerous, so don't try it unless it's an extreme emergency—and then, don't forget to keep your hands stretched out in front of you.

You know, I could keep going with this list, but Papa Pete ordered me a fresh root-beer float, and it just arrived, so I think you should finish the list yourself. Let me know what you come up with.

By the way, did I mention to you that I won a medal today? I'm pretty sure it's real gold. But even if it isn't, I'm so proud.

THE ZIPPITY END

About the Authors

HENRY WINKLER is an actor, producer, and director, and he speaks publicly all over the world. In addition, he has a star on Hollywood Boulevard, was knighted by the government of France, and the jacket he wore as the Fonz hangs in the Smithsonian Museum in Washington, D.C. But if you ask him what he is proudest of, he would say, "Writing the Hank Zipzer books with my partner, Lin Oliver."

He lives in Los Angeles with his wife, Stacey. They have three children named Jed, Zoe, and Max, and two dogs named Monty and Charlotte. Charlotte catches a ball so well that she could definitely play outfield for the New York Mets.

LIN OLIVER is a writer and producer of movies, books, and television series for children and families. She has written over one hundred episodes of television and produced four movies, many of which are based on children's books. She is cofounder and executive director of the Society of Children's Book Writers and Illustrators, an international organization of twenty thousand authors and illustrators of children's books.

She lives in Los Angeles with her husband, Alan. They have three sons named Theo, Ollie, and Cole. She loves tuna melts, curious kids, any sport that involves a racket, and children's book writers everywhere.